THE
FUNERAL
PARTY

LUDMILA ULITSKAYA

Schocken Books New York

~THE FUNERAL PARTY~

*Translated from the Russian
by Cathy Porter*

Translation edited by Arch Tait

Translation copyright © 1999 by Cathy Porter

All rights reserved under International and Pan-American
Copyright Conventions. Published in the United States by
Schocken Books, a division of Random House, Inc., New York.
Distributed by Pantheon Books, a division of Random House,
Inc., New York. Originally published in Russia as *Veselye
Pokhorony* by Vagrius, Moscow, in 1999. Copyright © 1999
by Ludmila Ulitskaya. This translation first published in Great
Britain by Victor Gollancz, an imprint of Orion Books Ltd.,
London, in 1999.

Library of Congress Cataloging-in-Publication Data

Ulitskaia, Liudmila.
　[Veselye pokhorony. English]
　The funeral party / Ludmila Ulitskaya ; translated from the
　Russian by Cathy Porter.
　　p. cm.
　ISBN 0-8052-4185-X
　　I. Porter, Cathy.　II. Title.

PG3489.2.L58 V4713 2001　　891.73′5—dc21　　00-059513

Schocken and colophon are registered trademarks of Random
House, Inc.

www.schocken.com

Book design by Johanna Roebas

Printed in the United States of America

First American Edition

9 8 7 6 5 4 3 2 1

THE
FUNERAL
PARTY

ONE

The heat was terrible, with one hundred per cent humidity. It was as if the whole of this great city, with its inhuman buildings, its magical parks, its different coloured people and dogs, had reached the point of a phase transition, and at any moment its semi-liquefied people would float up into the soupy atmosphere.

The shower was permanently occupied, with a queue of people standing outside. For a long time they hadn't bothered with clothes, although Valentina wore a bra to prevent her large breasts chafing in the heat; normally she never wore one. Everyone was dripping wet, the sweat failed to evaporate from their bodies, towels didn't dry, and hair had to be dried with a hair-dryer.

The blinds were half-open and strips of light fell across the floor. The air-conditioning hadn't worked in years.

There were five women in the bedroom: Valentina in her red bra, Nina with her gold cross and long hair, so thin that

Alik had once told her, "Nina you're as skinny as that snake-basket." (The basket stood in a corner of the room; when Alik was younger he had gone to India in search of ancient wisdom, but the basket was all he had brought back with him.)

Also present was their neighbour Gioia, a foolish Italian woman who had moved into the building hoping to learn some Russian in this strange environment. Gioia was forever taking offence with people, but since they never noticed her imaginary slights she always magnanimously forgave them.

Irina Pearson, formerly a circus acrobat, now a high-paid lawyer, looked stunning with her waxed bikini-line and a new bust constructed for her by an American surgeon to look no worse than her old one. With her was her fifteen-year-old daughter, Maika, known as Teeshirt ("maika" means teeshirt in Russian). A plump, clumsy girl in glasses, she was the only one of them wearing clothes. She had on a pair of wide Bermuda shorts and of course a teeshirt, depicting an electric light-bulb and a luminous message saying FUCKIT! in Russian. Alik had made it for her birthday the year before, when he still more or less had the use of his arms.

Alik himself lay on a wide divan-bed, looking as small and young as his own son. He and Nina had no children, however, and it was obviously too late for them to have any. A sort of slow paralysis was consuming the last vestiges of his musculature, and his limbs lay meek and inert, neither dead nor alive to the touch, but in some transitional state, like setting plaster. The most alive feature about him was his cheerful shock of red hair that stuck up in front of his head like a brush, and his straggly moustache which appeared enormous on his emaciated face.

This was his second week at home. He had told the doctors at the hospital that he didn't want to die there. There were other reasons for this which they didn't know, and which he didn't tell them. But even in this high-speed hospital—where the doctors treated their patients like fast food cooks, with never enough time to look into their eyes, only their rear-ends, or their throats or wherever it was that was wrong—everybody loved Alik.

His apartment on the sixth floor was like a general thoroughfare, crowded from morning to night with people. Some would end up staying the night and it was an excellent place for parties, but for normal life it was hopeless, an old rehabilitated loft warehouse with the end partitioned off to make a tiny kitchen, a lavatory and shower-unit, and a narrow bedroom with a slice of window. There was also a large studio with two light sources.

In a corner of the studio was a carpet on which late guests and stray visitors would sleep. Sometimes there were as many as five of them on it. There was no front door, and people came in directly from the service lift. Before Alik moved in, bales of tobacco used to be brought up in this lift, and its smell still hovered in the air. It was almost twenty years since Alik had first arrived. He had signed the lease without really looking at it, and it had proved exceptionally advantageous to him as he still paid next to nothing for the place, although it was generally someone else who paid; it was a long time since he had had any money.

The doors of the lift clattered and Fima Gruber walked in, pulling off his pale-blue work shirt. The near-naked women paid no attention to him, and he appeared not to notice them either. He carried with him his grandfather's old medical bag, which he had brought over from Kharkov in the Ukraine. Fima was a third-generation doctor, an educated and original man, but somehow things hadn't worked out for him; he still hadn't managed to pass his exams in this country, and for the past five years had had a temporary job as a kind of qualified lab assistant in an expensive private clinic. He came to see Alik every day in the hope that he might strike lucky and be able to help him.

He bent over him now: "How are you feeling, old man?"

"Oh, it's you. Have you brought the timetable?"

"The timetable?" Fima was puzzled.

"For the ferry." Alik smiled weakly.

It's all over, his mind's wandering, Fima thought, going to the kitchen and rummaging in the freezer compartment of the refrigerator for the ice-trays.

"Morons, they're all morons. I hate them," thought Maika. She had recently studied Greek mythology, and it was clear to her that Alik didn't have the South Ferry in mind.

Striding to the window with an angry, haughty expression, she lifted a corner of the blind and looked down at the street, where there was always something going on.

Alik was the first grown-up in her life to earn her respect. Like many American children, since early childhood she had been dragged from psychotherapist to psychotherapist, not without reason either, since she spoke only to other children, and was reluctant to make an exception even for her mother. Other adults didn't exist for her. The teachers at her school looked at her written work, clear, precise and laconic, shrugged their shoulders and gave her top marks. The psychotherapists thought up far-fetched theories to explain her strange behaviour; they loved unconventional children, they were their bread and butter.

Maika had met Alik at the opening of his exhibition. Irina had asked her clumsy daughter to accompany her soon after they moved to New York from California, and having suddenly lost all her friends, Maika agreed to go. Her mother had known Alik in her youth in Moscow, when she worked in the circus, but it was many years since they had last met in America, so many years that Irina had stopped wondering what she would say to him when they met again. When they did, he put his left hand on her jacket button, with a fat, shiny eagle which resembled a hen on it, twisted it sharply and tore it off. He threw it in the air and caught it, then opened his hand and glanced at it: "I've got to tell you something," he said.

His right hand hung lifelessly by his body. With his left hand he touched her thick, light-brown hair, each strand kept in place by a black silk bow edged with real pearls, and whispered in her ear: "Irka, I'm dying."

Oh, so you're dying, she thought; you died for me long ago. But a sharp blade twisted in the pit of her stomach, and she felt the pain running along the cut through to her spine. Maika stood nearby, watching her.

"Let's go back to my place," Alik said.

"I'm with my daughter. I don't know if she'll want to," Irina said, looking over at her.

Her little girl generally refused to go anywhere with her; she had barely managed to persuade her to come today.

"You want to come to my artist friend's studio?" she asked her now, convinced that she would refuse.

But Maika merely said, "The red-haired guy? Okay."

So they went. His new paintings reminded Irina of his old ones. A few days later they happened to be passing and called in again. At some point Irina was called to an urgent meeting and left Maika in the studio with Alik for a couple of hours. She returned to find them screeching at each other like two angry birds. Alik kept bobbing up and down, flapping his left arm; the right one was wasted and almost useless.

"Why can't you get it into your head that it's about asymmetry! That's all there is to it! Symmetry's death! A dead end! A short circuit!"

"Stop yelling!" shouted Maika blushing, every freckle on her face standing out, her American accent more pronounced than ever. "Maybe I just like symmetry! What are you going to do about it anyway? Why do adults always have to be right?"

Alik dropped his arm. "Well, you know . . ."

Irina almost passed out by the lift. Alik, without knowing it, had effortlessly dispelled the strange autism that had afflicted her daughter since she was five. An old flame of anger flickered inside her, then died down: why take Maika to psychotherapists, when she could offer her this human contact she so obviously needed?

TWO

The lift clattered again, and in the doorway of the studio Nina saw a new visitor. Pulling on her black kimono, she flew out to meet her.

A short, immensely fat old woman seated herself breathlessly in a low armchair and planted a bulging cloth shopping-bag between her feet. She was crimson and steaming, her cheeks gleamed like a samovar.

"Maria Ignatevna, over two days I've been waiting for you!"

The old woman sat on the edge of the chair spreading wide her pink feet in little slipper-socks of a kind not found on this continent. "I didn't forget you, dear, I've been working with Alik all this time. He was in my thoughts yesterday from six in the evening." She held up before Nina's face her crooked, distrophied hands with their greenish fingernails. "It's hypertension, dear, my blood pressure's up, I can barely walk. This wretched heat. Never mind, here's the last of them."

She fished out of her bag three large dark bottles containing a thick liquid. "I've mixed him these new oils for rubbing and inhaling. This one's for his feet. Put some on a cloth and wrap it round his feet, then tie a plastic bag on top and leave it for a couple of hours. Never mind if bits of skin peel off, just give him a good wash the minute you take it off."

Nina gazed raptly at this human scarecrow and her collection of remedies. Taking the smallest bottle she pressed it to her cheek to cool it, then carried them all into the bedroom, drew the blinds and set them on the narrow window-sill, where a battery of them already stood waiting.

Maria Ignatevna busied herself in the kitchen making tea; she was the only one of them who could drink it in this heat, not iced American tea, but hot Russian tea with jam and sugar.

Nina shook her long hair, whose gilt was wearing away to reveal a deeper silver underneath, and started putting compresses on Alik's feet. Then she covered his body with a thin bedspread of some fake, clanless Scottish tartan.

Maria Ignatevna was chatting with Fima, who wanted to know about her results.

She peered at him with benign contempt. "Results? Efim Isakich! Fima! What results! They smell of the earth. It's all in God's hands, that's what I say. I've seen it for myself—someone's going, they're just about to go, but no, He won't let them. There's power in those plants, they can go through rock. It's the top bit you need. I only use the top bit, even with the roots. A person's bent right down to the ground, next minute they're standing up right as rain! You must have faith in God, Fima. Without God even the plants won't grow!"

"I expect you're right," Fima said lightly, rubbing his left cheek, still pitted with the traces of hormonal battles of his youth.

In his fifth year of botany he had studied positive phototaxis, about which this woman with a face like a dishcloth uttered her vague and enigmatic pronouncements. But whatever skills he possessed as a doctor told him there was no hope for Alik and his cursed illness; his last working muscle, in his diaphragm, was already packing up. In the next few days death from asphyxiation would surely follow. The question for Americans in these cases—when to switch off the machine—had been settled ahead of time by Alik himself: he had left the hospital just before the end, and in so doing had refused the pathetic makeweight of an artificially prolonged life.

It depressed Fima to think that at some point he would probably be the one to administer to Alik the sedative which would ease the torment of asphyxiation, depressing his respiratory system as a side effect, and thereby killing him. But there was nothing to be done about it; calling for an ambulance to take him to the hospital, as they had done twice before, was out of the question now, and finding more false papers for him would be both risky and difficult.

"Good luck to you," he said softly to Maria Ignatevna, grabbing his bag and hurrying out without saying goodbye.

Maybe he was cross about something, Maria Ignatevna thought. She had little understanding of life in this country. She had been summoned from Byelorussia a year ago by a sick relative, but by the time she had filled in the forms and was ready to leave there was no one left to cure, so she crossed the ocean with her magic powers and contraband herbs for nothing. Not for nothing, in fact, because here too she found admirers of her craft, and she practised her unlawful and unlicensed healing activities without fear of the consequences. No one could tell her anything about taxes or licences, she was amazed by the way things were done here; she treated people, she snatched them from the other world—what did she have to fear?

When Nina first met her in the small Orthodox church in Manhattan, she knew immediately that God had sent this wisewoman to her for Alik. She had turned to the Church a year or two earlier, before he fell ill, thus dealing a severe blow to superstition, and deciding that her beloved Tarot cards were a sin, she had given them to Gioia.

Maria Ignatevna was now beckoning to her from the kitchen. She hurried in, poured orange juice into a glass, topped it up with vodka and threw in a handful of ice-cubes. She always drank the American way now: weak, sweet and ceaseless. She mixed it with a swizzle stick and took a gulp. Maria Ignatevna stirred her tea and laid the spoon on the table.

"Now you listen to me," she said sternly. "He must be baptized or nothing will work. I mean it."

"He doesn't want it, Maria Ignatevna, how many times do I have to tell you, he doesn't want it!" Nina flared up.

"No need to shout," Maria Ignatevna's eyebrowless face furrowed. "I'm going home soon anyway. My bit of paper's used up." (By this she meant her long-expired visa, but she could never remember a single foreign word.) "The paper's used up. In a couple of days I'm leaving, they've already punched my ticket. You must fetch the priest, otherwise I shall give up on him. If you do, I'll work with him, Nina, one way or another, even from back there. If not, there's no hope." She flung up her arms melodramatically.

"I can't do anything, he doesn't want it. He just laughs. Fine, he says, let your God take me, as I am unaffiliated with any party." Nina bowed her frail little head.

Maria Ignatevna opened her eyes wide. "What's wrong with you, girl? What does the good Lord care about the party?"

Nina waved dismissively and gulped the rest of her drink.

Maria Ignatevna poured herself more tea. "I'm sorry for you Nina, I really am. Our Lord has many mansions. I've seen lots of good people, even Jews, all sorts. He has a place for all of them. Take my Konstantin, may he rest in peace. He was baptized, and now he's waiting for me where all should be. I'm no saint, I lived with him for only two years and I was widowed at twenty-one. I got up to a few things, I admit it, I've sinned. But he was my only husband and now he's waiting for me there. Do you see what I'm getting at? If you want to be with him when you get there he has to be baptized, unconscious if need be."

"What d'you mean, unconscious?" Nina was taken aback.

"We must get away from everyone," Maria Ignatevna hissed. And although the others were gathered around Alik at that moment and the kitchen was empty, she pushed Nina into the lavatory. Here she sat on the pink seat-cover of the toilet, while Nina perched on the plastic laundry-box and listened to her instructions in this most inappropriate of settings.

Soon Faika arrived, strong as a nutcracker, with a woody face and pale wiry hair that stuck up like pieces of straw. She was one of the most recent arrivals in America, but she had acclimatized quickly.

"Hey, I've bought a new camera!" she announced from the door. Going over to Alik she waved the box above his motionless head. "It's a Polaroid with a reversible film! You're going to have your picture taken!"

There were many things in this country which Faika had yet to try, and she was in a hurry to buy everything, taste everything, check everything out and form opinions.

Valentina fanned Alik with the sheet, making a breeze over him, but he was the only one of them who wasn't too hot. Throwing the sheet aside, she slipped behind him and sat with her back against the headboard, pulling him up so that his dark auburn head rested on her solar plexus, where according to her late grandmother the "little soul" had its home. All of a sudden, tears of pity welled up for his poor head, lolling helplessly against her chest like a baby who hasn't yet learnt to hold it up. Never in their long affair had she felt such a keen, searing desire to hold him in her arms, to carry him, or better still to hide him in the depths of her body and protect him from this damnable death which had already so manifestly touched his arms and legs.

"Gather around girls, the cock has crowed!" she cried with a smile on her lips, hanging her celebrated breasts in their red packaging over Alik, and wiping the sweat from her forehead and the tears from her cheeks.

Gioia sat on one side of the bed, bending Alik's leg at the knee and holding it up with her shoulder. On the other side, for photographic symmetry, sat Teeshirt.

Faika turned the camera over, looking for the viewfinder. She finally squinted through it. "Oy Alik, your balls are in the way, cover them up!" she ordered.

The tubes of his urine-bag were in the foreground.

"Cover up such loveliness? What an idea!" Valentina snorted.

Alik twitched a corner of his mouth. "Precious little use for it now," he said.

"Wait, Faika," Valentina said. Pushing two large Russian cushions from Nina's trousseau behind his back, she moved down the bed and started gently peeling the pink plaster from the tender spot to which the catheter had been attached.

"Let him rest a bit and run free," she said.

Alik smiled; he liked jokes, even second-rate ones. Valentina worked quickly, with a practised hand; there are women, born nurses, whose hands know everything in advance and don't need to be taught.

Unable to bear any more, Maika jumped up and left the room. Last year she had had sex, first with Geoffrey Leshinsky then with Tom Caine, and she had come to the conclusion that she didn't need it for anything in the world. But for some reason she felt shaken by Valentina's ritual with the catheter, and the way she fingered him, and why were they all over him like that?

The shower happened to be free at that moment. As she stepped out of her shorts she felt the small rectangular box through the material. She wrapped everything up carefully, to make sure nothing fell out. She remembered every word of her instructions. She had spent last night beside Alik, not the whole night, just a few hours. Nina had gone off to sleep in the studio, but Alik hadn't slept; he had called for her, she had agreed to do everything he had asked, and now, that little box was proof that she really was the one who was closest to him.

The heat had warmed the water in the pipes, and all the towels were wet. Drying herself as best she could, she slithered into her clothes and slipped out of the apartment: she didn't want to be photographed with him, she knew that.

Going down to the Hudson River, she made for the ferry pier and thought about the one normal adult who as though to spite her was now about to die, leaving her alone again with the innumerable idiots—Russians, Jews, Americans—who had surrounded her since the day she was born.

THREE

⌒⌐ Something had happened to Alik's vision. Things disappeared and sharpened simultaneously. Densities altered and expanded. The faces of his friends became liquid, and objects flowing. But this flowing was pleasant rather than unpleasant, and revealed the connections between them in a new way. The corner of the room was cut off by an old ski, from which the dingy white walls ran off cheerfully in all directions. These undulations were halted by a female figure sitting cross-legged on the floor, touching the wall with the back of her head. This point, where her head touched the wall, was the most stable part of the picture.

Someone had raised the blinds and the light fell on the dark liquids in the bottles, shining green and gold on the window-sill. The liquids stood at different levels, and this xylophone of bottles suddenly recalled a youthful dream. In those years he had painted many still lifes with bottles. Thousands of bottles. Maybe more than he had drunk. No, he had drunk more. He smiled and closed his eyes.

But the bottles didn't go away: they stood there palely, like waving columns on the other side of his eyelids. He realized that this was important. The realization crept in slowly and hugely, like a loose cloud. Bottles, bottle rhythms. Music sounded. Scriabin's light-music. This had turned out on closer study to be thin, mechanical rubbish. He had gone on to learn about optics and acoustics, but these hadn't been the key to anything either. His still lifes weren't bad, just utterly irrelevant: he hadn't discovered the metaphysical still lifes of Morandi yet.

All those paintings had been blown away in the wind; none were left now apart from a few in Petersburg maybe, stored by his friends there, or by the Kazantsevs in Moscow. God, how they used to drink in those days. They had collected the bottles, taking back the ordinary empties, but the foreign ones and the old ones of coloured glass they kept.

The bottles standing on the tin flap which edged the roof of the Kazantsevs' house in Moscow were Czech beer-bottles of dark glass. No one could remember who had put them up there. In the Kazantsevs' kitchen was a low door leading up to the attic, and from the attic a window opened on to the roof. Irina once darted out of this window and ran across the roof. There was nothing unusual about this, they were forever running on to the roof to dance and sunbathe. This time she darted out and slid on her bottom down the pitch, and when she stood up two dark stains were clearly visible on the buttocks of her white jeans. She stood poised on the edge of the roof, his miraculous, light girl. God had sent them each other for their first love, and they were true and honest until the heavens rang.

Irina's strict grandfather, who was from an old circus family, had banished her from the troupe after she ran off with Alik to Petersburg for a couple of days and missed a rehearsal. They had moved into the Kazantsevs' attic together and lived there for the next three months, weak from the weight of their still growing feelings for each other.

On the day Irina ran across the roof they had had a visitor, a well-known writer of teenage fiction, a solid, grown-up man who brought two bottles of vodka with him. Irina liked him; she twitched her shoulders, lowered her eyelids, and when she spoke to him her voice was a little lower than usual.

"Why are you flirting like that?" Alik whispered. "It's cheap. If you like him, go ahead."

She really did like him.

"I didn't really, not in that way," she told Alik later. "Only a bit anyway."

But at the time, angry at the cruel truth of his words, she had jumped out of the window, slid on her bottom to the edge of the roof and stood up to her full height beside the bottles. Then squatting down on her heels—only Alik could see what she was doing—she grasped the necks of the first two bottles and kicked up her legs. The sharp toes of her shoes froze against the spreading lilac of the sky. Those facing the window saw her hand-stand and fell silent.

The writer, who could see nothing, chuckled at himself as he recounted a story about a general who had his overcoat stolen. Alik took a step closer to the window. Irina was already walking on her hands over the bottles now. She grasped the necks with both hands, tore one hand away, felt for the next bottle and grasped that one, transferring the weight of her tensed body on to it. The writer's bass voice rumbled on. Then, realizing that something was going on behind his back, he stopped and looked around. His fleshy cheeks trembled; he couldn't abide heights. The building was no more than one-and-a-half storeys—five metres high—but physiology is more powerful than arithmetic.

Alik's hands were wet. The sweat dripped down his back. Nelka Kazantseva, their landlady and another wild woman, clattered down the wooden stairs and dashed out on to the street.

Slowly, the points of her shoes scratching the petrified sky, Irina reached the last bottle, tucked her legs under her, landed gracefully on her toes and slid down a rickety drain-pipe.

Nelka was already standing outside. "Run! Run as fast as you can!" she yelled.

She had seen the expression on Alik's face, and her reaction was swift.

Irina rushed towards Kropotkin Subway Station, but it was too late. Alik caught up with her, grabbed her by the hair and slapped her face.

They stayed together for two more years after that because they didn't know how to finish it, but the best part had ended with that slap. Eventually they parted, unable to forgive or to stop loving each other. Their pride was diabolical: she had gone off with her writer that night and Alik hadn't turned a hair.

It was Irina who finally made the break. She was taken on by a troupe of trapeze artists, a rival company, which made her grandfather curse her, and she spent the whole of that summer on tour with the big top. Alik then made his first attempt to emigrate: he moved to Petersburg.

He opened his eyes. He could still feel the heat coming

off the hot roof of the Kazantsevs' shabby house in Afana-sevsky Street, and his muscles seemed to twitch in response to his headlong flight down the wooden stairs. In his dream the memories seemed richer than in his memory itself, for he could make out details which had long been obliterated: their landlord's cracked cup with the portrait of Karl Marx on it; the single aristocratic pure-white lock of hair on the dark head of the Kazantsevs' ten-year-old son; the ring with the dead-green turquoise in the dark-blue enamel setting on Irina's finger, which she had lost soon afterwards . . .

The sun was already setting over New Jersey, and the light slanted through the window on to Alik. He screwed up his eyes. Gioia was sitting on the bed beside him reading *The Divine Comedy*. She read in Italian at his request, inelegantly repeating each *terza* in English. Alik didn't tell her that he knew Italian rather well: he had lived in Rome for almost a year, and that happy, glass-clinking language had imprinted itself effortlessly on his mind like a handprint in clay. But none of his gifts had any meaning now: he would be taking with him his tenacious memory, his fine musical ear, his skill as an artist, along with his ridiculous talents for yodelling and playing a strong game of billiards.

Valentina was massaging his bloodless leg, and it seemed to her that a little life was coming back into the muscles.

While he was in this state of sleepy oblivion, Arkasha Libin arrived with a new air-conditioner and a reasonably new girlfriend, Natasha. Libin was an admirer of ugly women of a particular type: petite, with large foreheads and tiny mouths.

"Libin is approaching perfection," Alik had joked recently. "You'd have trouble fitting a teaspoon into Natasha's mouth. He'll have to feed the next one on spaghetti!"

Libin planned to remove the old broken air-conditioner and install the new one in a single day, and to do this alone, although even professionals generally worked in pairs. But Russian confidence is indomitable. Moving the bottles from the sill to the floor he took down the blinds, and the Latin-American music Alik so disliked instantly surged up from the street as if the window had been taken out. For two weeks now the block had been tormented by a band of six South American Indians who had picked this corner under his window to play their music.

"Can't someone shut them up?" he asked quietly.

"It's easier to shut you up," replied Valentina, clapping a pair of earphones to his ears.

Gioia looked at Valentina indignantly, offended this time for Dante too.

Valentina put on a tape of a Scott Joplin rag for Alik. He had taught her to listen to this music during their secret nocturnal walks around the city.

"Thanks, Bunny." He flickered his eyelids.

He called them all Pussy-cats and Bunnies. Most of them had arrived in this country with twenty kilograms of luggage and twenty words of English, leaving behind hundreds of ruptures large and small—with jobs, parents, streets and neighbourhoods. The rupture they were slowest to recognize was with their native language, which over the years became more and more instrumental and utilitarian. The new American language came to them gradually in their new emigré milieu and was also instrumental and primitive, and they expressed themselves in a terse, deliberately comical jargon, part-English, part-

22

Russian, part-Yiddish, which took in the most exotic criminal slang and the playful intonations of a Jewish anecdote.

"Oy, this isn't music, it's *koshmar*," Valentina grumbled. "Be an angel and shut your window. Do they think only about eat and drink, and have fun and get the good mood? They make such *gevalt* we get all the headache."

Gioia, offended, laid the red volume of her Florentine emigré on the bed and returned to her apartment next door. Small-mouthed Natasha brewed coffee in the kitchen. Valentina turned Alik on his side and rubbed his back; he had no bedsores so far. They didn't reattach the urine-bag, for the plasters flamed his skin.

Sodden sheets piled up, which Faika collected and took to the laundry on the corner. Nina dreamed in a chair in the studio, glass in hand. Libin fussed unsuccessfully with the air-conditioner; he didn't have the bracing slat he needed, and in the usual Russian way he was trying to make a short one out of two long ones so he wouldn't have to go home for the tools he had forgotten to bring with him.

FOUR

⌒After a long retreat, the sun finally slipped down like a
fifty-kopeck piece behind the bed, and a few minutes later it
was night. Everyone left, and for the first time that week Nina
had Alik to herself. Each time she went to him she was newly
appalled. A few hours of alcohol-fortified sleep rested her soul:
in sleep she blissfully forgot about this rare and peculiar dis-
ease which was draining the life from him with such terrible
power, and every time she awoke she hoped that the spell
would have passed and he would come to meet her with his
usual "How are you doing, Bunny rabbit?"

But he didn't.

She lay down beside him, covering his angular shoulder
with her hair. He seemed to be asleep. His breathing was shal-
low and irregular. She listened closely. Without opening his
eyes he said, "When will this damned heat end?"

She jumped up and ran to the corner of the room, where

24

Libin had arranged Maria Ignatevna's herbal masterpieces in seven bottles on the floor. Taking the smallest one and removing the cork, she pushed it under Alik's nose. It smelt of ammonia.

"Better? Is that better?" she asked urgently.

"A bit," he agreed.

She lay down beside him again, turned his head to face her and whispered in his ear: "Alik, do it for me, please, I beg you."

"Do what?" He didn't understand, or pretended not to.

"Get baptized, and everything will be all right. And the medicine will work." She took his weak hand in both of hers and gently kissed his freckled fingers. "And you won't be afraid."

"But I'm not afraid, my darling."

"So I can fetch the priest?"

Alik focused his wandering gaze and said, unexpectedly seriously: "Nina, I have no objection to your Jesus. I quite like him in fact, although his sense of humour isn't all it could be. The thing is, I'm a clever Jew myself. There's something silly about these sacraments. It's theatre, and I don't like theatre. I prefer the cinema. Leave me alone, Bunny rabbit."

Nina clasped her thin fingers together and waved them at him as though praying. "Please, won't you just talk to him? Let him come, you can talk."

"Let who come?" asked Alik.

"The priest of course. He's a very, very good man. I'm begging you . . ." Slowly she licked Alik's neck and his collarbone, then the nipple stuck to his ribcage, in a familiar inviting gesture they both understood. She was seducing him into baptism, turning it into an erotic game.

He smiled weakly at her. "Go on then, call your priest. Only on one condition: you must call a rabbi too."

Nina was nonplussed. "Are you joking?"

"Why should I joke? If you want me to take this serious step I've the right to a second opinion." Alik always knew how to derive the maximum pleasure from every situation.

But Nina was satisfied. "He agreed, he agreed!" she said to herself. "He'll be baptized."

Everything had been arranged in advance with the priest at Nina's little Orthodox church. An educated man, descended from emigrés who had fled the 1917 revolution, Father Victor had a complicated life-story and a simple faith. He was a sociable, humorous character who liked to drink and was always happy to visit his parishioners.

Where rabbis were to be found, Nina had no idea. Their circle of Jewish friends had no connections with the religious community, and she would have to devote much effort to finding one if these were Alik's terms.

For the next two hours she busied herself with her bottles, putting more compresses on Alik's feet and rubbing his chest with an acrid-smelling infusion. It was three in the morning when she remembered Irina laughing as she told them she must be the only one of them who knew how to cook gefilte fish, because she had once been married to a proper Jew who kept kosher and the Sabbath and the rest of it.

She dialled Irina's number.

When Irina received Nina's call in the middle of the night, she froze; it's over, she thought.

"Listen, Ira, was your husband a religious Jew?" Nina's wild voice demanded through the mouthpiece.

She must be drunk, Irina thought.

"He certainly was," she replied.

"Could you get hold of him for me please? Alik needs a rabbi."

No, she's just mad, Irina decided.

"We'll talk about it tomorrow," she said carefully. "It's three in the morning, I'm not phoning anyone at this hour!"

"Please Irina, it's important," Nina said in a completely clear voice.

"I'll come round tomorrow, okay?" Irina said, hanging up.

Irina had felt a deep curiosity about Nina. This may have been the real reason she agreed to go to Alik's studio one-and-a-half years ago, to see for herself this miracle in feathers that had got him.

Since the day he was born, women had always adored Alik. At kindergarten he was his teachers' pet. Later at school, all the girls would invite him to their birthday parties and would fall in love with him, along with their grandmothers and their grandmothers' dogs. In his teenage years, when people are driven crazy with impatience for adult life to begin, and good little girls and boys rush into ridiculous adventures, Alik was indispensable: he listened to his friends' confessions and was able to laugh at them and make them laugh at themselves. But his most rare and precious quality was his confidence that life would begin next Monday and that yesterday could be erased, especially if it hadn't been totally successful. At the School of Performing Arts, where he was a student, even the inspector of his course, known as Snake Venom, proved susceptible to his charms. Four times he was expelled, and three times, thanks to her efforts, he was taken back.

Nina struck Irina at their first meeting as a silly woman, stuck-up and capricious. Before her in the studio she saw a faded beauty seated on a dirty white carpet, doing a giant jigsaw puzzle and asking not to be disturbed. On closer acquaintance she turned out to be merely simple-minded, and psychologically unbalanced too; inertia alternated with hysteria, bouts of joy with melancholy.

She understood why Alik had married her, but he had obviously had to put up with years of her mind-numbing silliness, pathological laziness and muddle. Irina felt not so much retrospective jealousy as a deep sense of puzzlement. She had never come across Nina's type before. Her infinite helplessness clearly aroused in others, particularly men, feelings of heightened responsibility. She had another trait too: each of her whims, caprices and weaknesses she took to the limit. For instance, she refused to touch money, so that if Alik went to Washington for a week he would have to fill the fridge with food before he left, knowing that she wouldn't go to the store and would rather starve than handle filthy banknotes. As well as this Nina never cooked, because she was afraid of fire. In Russia she had been keen on astrology, and had read that as a Libra she was in danger from fire. From then on she never went near the stove, fearful of the cosmic incompatibility of the air and fire elements. Here in Alik's studio, where the stove was not gas but electric, and the only living flame she ever came into contact with was at the end of a match, her aversion to cooking remained as strong as ever, and Alik learned to be a successful and imaginative cook.

Apart from money and fire there was something else,

something more intangible, an insane, senseless fear of making decisions. The more insignificant the decision, the more Nina anguished over it. Irina once received some free opera tickets from a client who was a singer, and at Maika's request they invited Alik and Nina along. They arrived to pick them up and witnessed Nina's indecision as she tried on endless little black dresses and smart shoes, finally flinging herself on the bed, sobbing into the pillow and refusing to go, until Alik, avoiding the eyes of the involuntary onlookers, picked a dress at random and said: "Wear this one Nina, velvet and the opera go together like beer and sausages."

Maika evidently enjoyed this spectacle far more than she enjoyed the rather mediocre opera.

Irina knew perfectly well the value of such antics; her youth had been full of them. But unlike Nina she had the circus school behind her. Tightrope-walking is a very valuable skill for an emigré, and perhaps this explained why she was the most successful of them. The soles of the feet hurt, the heart almost stops, the sweat pours into the eyes, but the muscles stretch to a wide, all-purpose smile, the chin tilts victoriously, the tip of the nose points to the stars—light and easy, easy and light.

For eight years she had skipped precisely two hours of sleep every night, fighting tooth and nail for her expensive American profession. And now she had to make ten decisions a day and had long since learned not to get too upset if today's proved not to be the best. "The past is definitive and irreversible, but it has no power over the future," she would say at such times. And suddenly it turned out that her irreversible past did have power over her.

Irina had had no discussions with Alik about his impending death or his past life, but what she hadn't dared to dream about had taken place; her little girl talked with him and his friends so easily and freely that none of them had any idea of the complex psychological disorder she had suffered. And now Irina couldn't explain to herself how she too had spent almost every free minute of her time for the last two years in his noisy, disorderly lair.

An English goldfish named Doctor Harris (he looked more like a sunburnt tunny than a delicate veiltail), whom Irina had been discreetly dating for four years, had just visited New York for five days, almost failed to reach her and flown out disappointed, convinced that she was planning to drop him. But dropping him didn't come into Irina's plans. Harris was a renowned authority on copyright law. His status was such that in the normal course of events she would never have met him, and it was by sheer chance that one of the partners at her law firm decided to take her with him to England for a business meeting. Afterwards there was a party at which virtually no women were present, and she shone against the black dinner-jackets like a dove in a flock of crows. Two months later, after she had forgotten about the trip, she received an invitation to attend a conference of young lawyers. Her boss was at a loss to explain it, but could hardly suspect Harris of taking an interest in his diminutive assistant. He had let her go to Europe for three days. And now it turned out that Harris wanted to get married. It wasn't just self-interest either, it was serious.

Every woman who has turned forty dreams of a Harris, and Irina had just turned forty.

It was all rather foolish really.

The following evening Irina arrived to see Nina. Old Maria Ignatevna was in the bedroom, having called in for five minutes before her flight. Nina was scurrying around after her. The studio was filled with people as usual.

Irina was hungry. She opened the fridge. There wasn't much in there, just some expensive black bread wrapped in paper from the Russian grocer and a lump of stale cheese. She made a sandwich and drank some of Nina's vodka and orange; everyone was drinking screwdrivers in this house for some reason. Finally Nina slipped out of the bedroom.

"So what do you want Gottlieb for?" Irina asked.

"Who's Gottlieb?" Nina looked baffled.

"Oh Lord, Nina, have you forgotten? You called me last night!"

"Oh that, I didn't know his name. Alik said we must get him a rabbi," Nina said innocently.

Irina felt a surge of irritation and wondered why she bothered with this imbecile, but she contained herself and asked in a professional tone: "Why a rabbi? Are you sure you haven't made a mistake?"

Nina beamed. "You don't know anything! He's agreed to get baptized!"

Irina burst out: "But Nina, you need a priest to do that!"

"That's right, a priest," Nina nodded. "I know. I've already arranged it. But Alik asked . . . he wants to talk to a rabbi too."

"He wants to be baptized?" Irina said in amazement, finally understanding.

Nina dropped her narrow face into her bony, no longer

beautiful hands. "Fima says it looks bad. Everyone says it looks bad. Maria Ignatevna says it's his only hope now. I don't want him to go off into nowhere, I want God to accept him. You can't imagine what the darkness is like, it's impossible to describe . . ."

Nina knew something about the darkness, having made three suicide attempts herself, one in her early youth, the second when Alik left Russia, and the third in America after her baby was stillborn.

"We must do it quick." She poured the remains of the orange juice into her glass. "Bring me more juice will you, Irina? We're all right for vodka, Slavik bought some yesterday. Just get your Gottlieb over here with the rabbi."

Irina picked up her handbag and put her hand into the metal cruet on top of the fridge where the bills were kept, but it was empty: someone had already paid them.

FIVE

Irina told people she had backed every horse, including the Jewish one. The Jewish one was large, black-bearded Leva Gottlieb, who had pushed Russian Irina into Judaism. Not bits and pieces of Judaism either but virtually the full programme, with Sabbath candles, the ritual bath and the headgear, which happened to suit her very well. She was a Jew for two years; Maika was sent to a religious girls' school, of which she still had fond memories, and Irina studied Hebrew. She was an able student, and it came easily to her. She went to synagogue and enjoyed family life. Then one morning she woke up and realized she was bored stiff. She packed a few things and went off with her daughter, leaving Leva a note consisting of two words: "I've gone."

He tracked her down to some old friends of hers, and when he asked her why she had broken up the family, she replied only: "Boredom, Leva, boredom."

It was her last extravagant act, maybe her last act of emo-

33

tional defiance: she never allowed herself to do anything like it again.

She moved to California. How she lived in these years was a mystery to her New York friends. Some suspected she had had a stash, others that she might be living off a lover, no one could work it out. By day she wore her English silk and linen suits, and at night she stuck on her feathers and sequins and performed her acrobatic act at a special club frequented by rich idiots. The circus school was a proper profession, not just some PhD. Thanks to this profession, at night she would twirl her legs, and by day she would toil away at law school. In those years she learned to get up every morning at six-thirty, take a three-minute shower instead of her usual forty-minute bath, and not to pick up the phone until the machine had told her who it was. She eventually finished her studies and graduated, and got a job as assistant to one of the partners at a reputable Los Angeles law practice.

She had little contact with emigré circles in Los Angeles and she spoke American with a slightly English accent, on which she still had some work to do; it was rather chic in fact, but people who understand these things know that it is easier to lose one's Russian accent altogether than to replace an English with an American one. She also expediently changed her uncomplicated Russian surname when applying for her American papers.

She still had a few connections from her show career, and she brought several new clients to the practice. God knows what kind of clients they were, but her boss valued them. Before long he allowed her to handle a few small cases on her own, and she started winning them for him. For a young American her career would be considered pretty good; for a forty-year-old former circus acrobat from Russia it was brilliant.

For Leva too the divorce turned out to be for the best. He married a nice Jewish girl from Mogilev, who didn't have the experience of the circus behind her, or any other kind of experience either. Large, plump and wide-hipped, she bore him five children in seven years, which fully reconciled him to the loss of Irina.

His sensible wife would say to her friends: "You know our men fancy shiksas, but not after they find themselves a proper Jewish wife!"

This was the limit of her wisdom, but Leva wouldn't have disagreed with it.

Irina found him without difficulty in the telephone directory. When she asked him to meet her urgently he was greatly taken aback, and in the two hours it took her to reach him in the Bronx he anxiously awaited some major unpleasantness, or at least inconvenience, from her.

His office was rather shabby. The business he did there had been hatched by Irina, whose practical mind and easygoing attitude to money had served him well during their brief marriage. It was she who at the start of it had persuaded him to invest all his money, his laboriously accumulated five thousand dollars, in a high-risk kosher cosmetics business. This had proved to be brilliantly profitable. Irina was still in the throes of her short-lived love affair with Judaism then, a gentle, reformed Judaism to be sure, but one which respected the dramatic connection between milk and meat, especially meat which had oinked when alive.

Leva's cosmetics were just starting to find their market when Irina, plastered in non-kosher all-American cosmetics, walked out on him. As he embarked on this new phase of his life he quickly changed orientation and betrayed reformism for orthodoxy. There was a political reason he had to stop producing the crude paints which had defiled the noble faces of Jewish women, and sold this part of his business to his cousin, reserving for himself the production of kosher soaps and shampoos. He also learned to make kosher aspirin and other drugs, and he had plenty of customers, who evidently didn't regard the idea as a complete swindle.

Leva met Irina at the door to his office. Both were greatly changed, but these changes weren't so much to do with the passing of time as with the new directions their lives had taken. Leva had filled out, his jowls were fleshier and his back broader, which made him appear shorter; his face had lost the pink and white hue of the young King David, and he had acquired a sallow complexion. Irina, who during their marriage used to go around in knitted jerseys with holes on the shoulder and long Indian skirts which swept the floor, dazzled him now with her impeccable, fashion-plate looks, the sculpted elegance of her brows and nose, her firm chin and soft lips.

"A pearl, a real pearl," he thought, and said it out loud.

Irina laughed, her old light laugh. "I'm glad you like me, Leva, you don't look bad either, you're a serious, important-looking man now!"

"I've five children, Irina, five." He pulled a small photograph album from his desk. "So how's Maika?"

"She's fine, she's a big girl already." Irina examined the album and nodded, then put it back on the desk. "The thing is, an old friend, a Jew, someone I used to know in Moscow, is very ill. He's dying. He wants to talk to a rabbi. Could you arrange it?"

"Is that all?" Leva felt hugely relieved. He had imagined

she might make some financial claim to those five thousand dollars from the time they were married. He was a good man but he was burdened by family worries, and he hated unexpected expenses. "I can get you ten if you need it."

Immediately he had said it he felt embarrassed, but Irina didn't notice, or pretended not to. "It's urgent, he's terribly ill," she said.

Leva promised to call her that evening.

He did indeed call that evening, and told her that he would be bringing round a well-known rabbi from Israel who was delivering a course of erudite lectures at New York University; he agreed to bring him to the sick man as soon as the Sabbath was over.

It was uncharacteristic of Irina, who never forgot anything, to forget that the Jewish Sabbath ended on Saturday evening and she told Nina the rabbi would be coming on Sunday morning.

The priest, Father Victor, promised to visit on Saturday after early vespers. Nina attached great importance to the fact that the priest was coming first.

SIX

Fima visited Berman very late, without calling him first, this familiarity being usual between them. They were connected by old friendship. There was a distant family connection too, on their grandfather's side, but this wasn't important: what was important was that they had both been born doctors, in the sense that it pleases nature for someone to be born blond, or a singer, or a coward.

With these two it was a feeling for the human body, a sense of the circulation of the blood, a particular way of thinking: something systemic, as Berman put it. Both could spot the particular idiosyncrasies linked to a certain type of metabolism, which predisposed someone to high blood pressure, ulcers, cancer, asthma. At the start of a medical examination they would observe whether the skin was dry, the white of the eye dull, the corners of the mouth enflamed.

In recent years they rarely examined anyone, however, unless requested to by friends.

Unlike Fima, Berman had passed all the American medical exams and validated his Russian qualifications two months after he arrived, thereby setting a local record: no one had yet completed the medical course so quickly. He immediately found a job in one of the city's hospitals. He became acquainted with American medical practice, devoting seventy hours a week to it, and it appeared to him just as unsatisfactory as medicine in Russia, although for different reasons. After this he discovered a field which enabled him to keep his distance from American doctors, for he had little respect for them. It was a new field, recently invented, called radio-medicine, a diagnostic procedure which involved passing radioisotopes through the organism, and was followed up by a computer analysis.

In Russia they wouldn't have it for twenty years, he thought ruefully, maybe never.

Berman often said that he had used up what was left of his brains on mastering the skill to operate his new computer, his energy on raising the money to pay for it and open his diagnostic laboratory, and expected to spend what was left of his life on repaying the enormous debts he had achieved as a result. His work nevertheless went well, the business grew, increasing its turnover. For the time being, however, all of his income went on covering the interest on his loans, which in this country grew quickly and imperceptibly, like mildew across a damp wall. "We live like the rest of America," he would grin, clapping Fima on the shoulder.

Berman's debts were over four hundred thousand dollars. Fima's were four hundred dollars. In other words, according to American logic, the first prospered and the other lived in penury. In fact they both lived in identically shabby apartments and ate the same cheap food, the only difference being that while Fima dressed like a tramp, Berman bought himself three respectable "doctor's" suits.

Both knew that if lenders judged Berman's brains, education, or speculative business project to be that creditworthy, then it was no more than his due; he could have moved to the fashionable Upper East Side of Manhattan if he hadn't been so cautious with money.

Fima hunched into himself. It wasn't exactly envy he felt, but something morbid stirred in his soul. To be fair, when Berman opened his laboratory he had offered him work as his lab assistant. But Fima would have had to take various special courses for this, and he was still poring over his English textbooks trying to convince himself that next year he would finally mobilize himself to take his damned exams. In a word, the amiable offer was refused; to accept would have meant his total and final capitulation.

Years ago in Russia they had been equals, two talented young doctors who knew their worth. Here, thanks to Fima's inability to get his tongue round this damned language, Berman had shot so far ahead that Fima could never catch up with him. Now with Alik they were equals as before, two doctors attending the same patient.

Their meeting that night in Alik's kitchen was actually more of a consultation. Alik had turned first to Fima when his right arm started letting him down two years ago.

"It's nothing, just professional exhaustion—tendonitis probably," was Fima's first diagnosis. He had to revise this opinion when Alik's left arm also started to seize up. If it hadn't happened so suddenly Fima might have suspected multiple sclerosis. As it was, major tests were needed.

The first set of tests were carried out by Berman, free of

charge, naturally; he even paid for the isotopes. Nothing showed up on the computer.

"It's American, it won't work for nothing!" Berman grimaced. "Better buy yourself some health insurance old man, while you still look okay. It'll be valid in six months, you'll need it, I guarantee, these things don't just pass."

Alik had no money for insurance, and he never thought about what was going to happen in six months' time. This, plus his dislike of queues, forms and officials left over from Soviet times, was the reason he had never had any American benefits. While some of his fellow-emigrés vied to cadge as many hand-outs as possible, from food stamps to free rent, Alik had managed to live for almost two decades as free as air, working away on his own and out of sight and giving many of those who didn't know him well the impression that he merely improvised as he went along. The people he annoyed most were not the honest grafters but the inveterate scroungers.

In short, he had never had a regular job or any insurance either, and there was no prospect of him getting either now: this was no time for him to be queuing for days in endless corridors and collecting the necessary paperwork.

Fortunately the computerized, efficient American health service left a few gaps, and his first tests were on someone else's papers. The blood analysis showed nothing.

His first hospitalization was organized on the sidewalk: a little spectacle was staged, an ambulance was called. The owner of the café across the street from Alik's building called the hospital, saying that a man had collapsed unconscious by his door. Lying across three chairs, dangling his auburn ponytail and winking at his friend the café-owner, Alik waited five minutes for the ambulance. He was driven off, examined, and treated on Medicaid by neuropathologists, who attached him to tubes and prescribed drugs. The hospital was depressing, and Alik discharged himself. Fima shouted at him: the prescriptions were fine, they were treating the symptoms, what more could they do without a diagnosis? Fima insisted he go back, and the only way to do this was to cook something up. He quickly arranged a small fistula on Alik's collar-bone, and Alik announced that his condition had deteriorated after his unsuccessful treatment. The city hospital, although not private, disliked lawsuits and took him back.

It dragged on. Alik returned to hospital and discharged himself again. It wasn't clear if the treatment helped, or how he would have been without it. His right arm hung lifeless, with the left he could barely lift a spoon to his mouth. His gait changed. He became tired. He stumbled. Then he fell for the first time. It all happened with frightening speed. The following spring he was barely able to move.

Alik's second hospitalization was more difficult. He was taken to Berman's laboratory and Berman himself called for the ambulance, saying that he had a seriously ill patient at reception. The ambulance demanded a written undertaking that the patient wouldn't die on the journey. Berman, who knew all the bureaucratic tricks in this country, had already written it and accompanied Alik to the hospital. By a stroke of luck the nurse in charge turned out to be a friend of his, an old Irishwoman, frowning, abrupt, and a perfect angel. She sent them to the Chinese hospital, which was considered the best of the city's state institutions. This was a good move. As well as the usual drugs Alik was given acupuncture and moxa, and in the first week he perked up a little and it even seemed as though some of the feeling returned to his arm.

Now Fima sat with Berman in Alik's dingy kitchen with

the dirty cups and happy cockroaches. They had already run out of hypotheses: amyotrophic lateral sclerosis, a viral infection, some mysterious tumour.

Berman was rather good-looking, but there was something of the ape about him with his strong, stooping shoulders, his short inflexible neck and long arms; even his mouth was stretched tightly over his large teeth. Fima was all rough and gnarled; bright clear eyes looked expectantly at Berman out of his pitted face.

"It's hopeless, Fima. There's nothing to be done in these cases, just the oxygen mask."

"Asphyxiation may progress slowly and painfully," Fima frowned.

"Give him morphine, or whatever."

"Right," Fima muttered.

He had hoped clever Berman might know something he had forgotten, but such knowledge didn't exist.

SEVEN

Father Victor arrived at about nine, without socks and in sandals, carrying an attaché case and a bulging plastic bag. He was wearing a baggy shirt tucked into light, shortish trousers and a baseball cap with the innocuous letters "N" and "Y" on it.

He took off the cap as he came in and rested it on the crook of his arm, greeting everyone with a smile which wrinkled up his short nose.

Because it was Saturday there was a large number of visitors: Valentina, Gioia with a little grey Dostoyevsky under her arm, Irina, Maika, Faika, Libin and his girlfriend, all the usual crowd. Also present were the Beginsky sisters, recently arrived from Washington, a woman from Moscow whom nobody knew, and who said her name so indistinctly they couldn't hear it, Alik's American artist friend Rudy, who had worked with him on some joint project, Shmuel from Odessa with a dog named Kipling which he was looking after for a few days for an old friend.

Alik was lifted from the bed and seated in his usual place in the armchair, propped up on all sides with pillows. Everyone circled around the room, talking loudly and drinking. On the table stood various offerings: a large pecan pie, some ice-cream. It was more like a private view than the room of a dying man.

Father Victor seemed lost for a moment. Then Nina grabbed his elbow which was supporting the baseball cap, and sat him down at the table.

"My heart, which longs so much for pea-eace . . . !" crooned Shmuel, almost drowning out the Paraguayan pipes and drums tirelessly banging away under the windows.

Faika clasped a long, limp puppet which represented Alik. This prophetic doll had been given to him once on his birthday by his friend Anka Kron, who now lived in Israel. Alik gave the puppet its lines: "Oy, don't wink at me like that! In the name of God, Faika, have you been eating garlic?"

The priest smiled, took the puppet from Faika's hands, and shook its pink hand: "Pleased to meet you!"

Everyone laughed, and Father Victor put the puppet back on Faika's knee. Nina nodded. Shmuel was instantly silent. Libin lightly lifted Alik out of his chair and carried him like a child back to the bedroom.

The woman from Moscow shrank back: it was a pitiful sight. While Alik was sitting or lying down everything seemed normal, a sick man surrounded by his friends. But when he was moved from one place to another it was immediately apparent that something terrible was happening. The bright, lively eyes and the dead body. At the beginning of spring he had been able to move on his own from the studio to the bedroom.

Alik was put to bed, and Father Victor went into his room. Nina hovered around for a while, then slipped out and sat on the floor with her back to the door and a watchful, remote expression on her face; she was half-drunk, but composed.

This is totally stupid and pointless, Alik thought. He seems like a nice man, I should never have agreed to do it.

Father Victor sat on the stool, and leaned closer to Alik. "I am facing a number of professional difficulties here," he began unexpectedly. "You see, most people I meet, my parishioners, are convinced that I can solve their problems, and that if I don't it's purely for their own good, as a sort of lesson. They are entirely mistaken." He smiled a gap-toothed smile and Alik realized the priest understood the whole ridiculousness of the situation, and relaxed.

Alik's illness caused him no physical pain. He suffered from increasing breathlessness and an unendurable sense of dissolving self. Along with the weight of his body and the living flesh of his muscles, the reality of life was slipping away, which was why he took such pleasure in the half-naked women clinging to him from morning to night. It was a long time since he had seen any new people around him, and this unfamiliar face, with its flecked, greenish-brown eyes, carelessly shaved right cheek and small, western-style beard, impressed itself on his memory in photographic detail.

"Nina wanted me to talk to you," the priest went on. "She thinks I can baptize you, or, rather, persuade you to be baptized. I could not refuse her request."

The Paraguayan music outside the window howled, rattled and gave up the ghost, then came back to life again. Alik frowned. "I'm not a believer, you know, Father Victor," he said sadly.

"Stop, stop, what are you saying?" the priest waved an arm. "There are practically no non-believers. It's just a psychological cliché you brought over with you from Russia. I assure you there are no non-believers, particularly among artistic people. The nature of faith varies—the greater the intellect, the more complex the form it takes. There's also a form of intellectual chastity which won't allow anything to be discussed or articulated. We're surrounded by the most vulgar forms of primitive religiosity, and it's hard to bear . . ."

"I'm aware of that, I have my wife here," Alik replied. Father Victor's seriousness had endeared itself to him. He's not stupid either, he thought with surprise. Nina's ecstatic remarks about the wise priest had always grated on him, but now his irritation vanished.

"For Nina, as for other women," the priest gestured towards the door, "things pass not through the mind but through the heart, through love. They're marvellous beings, miraculous, astonishing . . ."

"You love women, don't you, Father Victor? So do I," Alik spurred him on.

The priest appeared not to understand him. "Yes, I'm terrible about them, almost all of them," he confessed. "My wife is always saying if it wasn't for my vocation I'd be a real womanizer."

What a simpleton, Alik thought.

But the priest warmed to his theme: "They're extraordinary, they're ready to sacrifice everything for love. At the centre of their lives is often love for a man—yes, there's this substitution. But sometimes, just occasionally, I meet one of those rare women in whom possessive, insatiable human love is transformed, and through the everyday, the ordinary, they come to the love of God Himself. It never ceases to amaze me. Your

Nina is one of those people, I think. I saw it as soon as I walked in today. You have so many beautiful women around you, so many good faces. Your friends aren't leaving you. Beneath the surface they are all like the women at the tomb of our Lord . . ."

Father Victor wasn't old, a few years the wrong side of fifty perhaps, yet his speech had an exalted, old-fashioned ring to it; he must be from the first, pre-war wave of emigration, Alik thought.

His movements were distracted and rather awkward. Alik liked that too. "It's a pity we didn't meet before," he said.

"Yes, yes, it's hot," the priest responded irrelevantly, not wanting to abandon the female theme which so inspired him. "You know, one could write a dissertation on it—the different forms faith takes among men and women . . ."

"I'm sure some feminist has already done it," Alik said. "Father Victor, would you please ask Nina to bring us two Margaritas? You like tequila?"

"I guess so," the priest replied uncertainly.

He stood up and opened the door a little. Nina was still sitting there, with a burning question mark in her eyes.

"Alik wants a Margarita," Father Victor told her. She didn't understand immediately. "Two Margaritas."

A moment later she was back carrying two large wine-glasses. She went out again, shooting a bemused look over her shoulder.

"So, shall we drink to women?" Alik suggested in his usual friendly, sardonic tone. "You'll have to hold the glass for me."

"Of course, with pleasure." Father Victor clumsily pushed the straw into his mouth.

He had seen a lot in his life, but nothing like this. He had

48

heard people's dying confessions, he had given them communion and even baptized some, but he had never given them tequila.

He put his own glass on the floor and continued: "With men, faith generally takes the form of battle. Remember Jacob's wrestling in the night with the angel? The struggle for oneself, rising up to a higher level. In that sense I'm an evolutionist. Salvation is too utilitarian an idea, wouldn't you agree?"

It seemed to Alik that the priest had got slightly drunk. Alik couldn't see that he hadn't in fact touched his drink. He himself felt a warmth in his stomach, and it was a pleasant feeling; he had fewer and fewer feelings nowadays.

"I believe the venerable Serafim Sarovsky called this battle for faith the seizing of the Holy Spirit. Yes . . ." Father Victor fell into a sad and thoughtful silence; at moments like these he realized clearly that he hadn't the spiritual vocation his grandfather had had.

The South American music wearied of itself and stopped, and was replaced by a good, human noise outside the window.

How weak I am, Alik thought.

This brave, simple-hearted man had touched him somehow. Why did he give the impression of being brave? He would have to think about it. Was it because he wasn't afraid of appearing ridiculous?

"Nina keeps begging me to get baptized. She pleads and weeps, it's terribly important for her. For me it's just a formality."

"What are you saying? I find her reasons entirely convincing. But I simply don't . . ." Father Victor threw up his arms in confusion, as though embarrassed by his privileges.

"You see, I know for sure that between us a Third is present."
He became even more embarrassed and fidgeted on his stool.

A mortal weariness came over Alik. He couldn't feel any
Third present; this Third was something out of a fairy-tale,
and it pained him that his foolish Nina felt it, and this simple-
hearted priest felt it, and he didn't feel it, sensing its absence
with the same sharpness, perhaps, as they sensed its presence.

"But I'm prepared to do it for her," he closed his eyes
from deathly tiredness.

Father Victor wiped the sweaty base of his glass on his
trousers and put it down on the table.

"I don't know, I really don't know. I can't refuse you,
you're so ill, but something's not right. Let me think. I know,
let's pray together. As best we can." Opening his attaché case,
he pulled out his vestments, slipped his surplice and stole over
his clothes, slowly tying the fastenings. Then he kissed the
heavy priestly cross, blessed by his late grandfather, and put it
around his neck. As he did so he seemed to grow older, state-
lier. Alik lay with closed eyes and didn't witness this transfor-
mation. The priest turned to a small faded print of the
Vladimir virgin tacked to the wall, then bowed his balding
head and prayed: "Help me, Lord, oh help me!"

At such moments he always remembered himself as a
small boy, standing on the football pitch behind the Russian
children's foster home outside Paris which his grandparents
had run during the war, and where he had spent the whole of
his childhood. And once again he was standing inside the
tattered rope squares of the goal where they sent him, the
youngest, when they had no proper goalkeeper, and he waited,
terrified, knowing that he would be unable to stop a single ball.

EIGHT

⌒Large Leva Gottlieb, with his shiny, black beard, ush-
ered respectfully out of the lift a thin, handsome man, also tall
and bearded, identical to Leva only four times narrower, like
his reflected image in a distorting mirror. Irina practically burst
out laughing, but she quickly regained her composure. Leva
spotted her at once in the throng and pushed towards her, ad-
dressing her like an irritable husband: "I said I'd call you after
the end of the Sabbath but your machine was on, it's a good
thing I wrote down your address . . ."

Irina clapped her hand to her forehead: "Jesus, I completely forgot that was Saturday evening! I thought it was tomorrow morning!"

Leva threw up his arms, then remembered the rabbi
standing beside him. The rabbi's face was both stern and curi-
ous; he didn't know a word of Russian.

Maika stood by the table holding a paper plate with a
large slice of pie, and stared at Leva. He charged at her like a

wild boar and grasped her head: "Hi, mouse!" He kissed the head of this grown-up girl who had lived for two years in his house, whom he had sat on the potty, taken to nursery and called "daughter."

"He's shameless, completely shameless," she thought, holding her head tensely in his stony grip. "I used to miss him so much, now I couldn't care less. They're morons, the lot of them!" She jerked her proud head and Leva sensitively released his grip.

The rabbi was dressed formally in a worn black suit of a perennially old-fashioned cut, and a huge fancy-dress silk hat, which you could tell was fated to be sat on by every new arrival. Beneath its crooked brim, two thick, unharvested sheaves of hair dangled luxuriantly from his temples, refusing to lie in neat spirals. He smiled into his music-hall beard, and said in English: "Good evening."

"Reb Menashe," Leva introduced him. "He's from Israel."

Just then the bedroom door opened and Father Victor came out in his surplice. He was pink and sweating, his eyes sparkled.

Nina threw herself at him. "What happened?"

"Don't worry, Nina. I'll come back . . . Just read the Gospel with him."

"He's read it, he's read it. I thought you'd do it for him now!" Nina was annoyed; she was used to having her wishes carried out immediately.

"Right now he's asking for another Margarita," Father Victor smiled ruefully.

Seeing the priest, Leva gripped Irina's wrist. "What is the meaning of this? Is it some kind of joke?"

Irina recognized this ferocious look and understood before he did his sudden desire for her; she remembered how lovemaking with him was always best when she annoyed him first with some taunt or slight.

"No, it isn't a joke, Leva." She gazed serenely into his eyes, holding back her smile and the wicked urge to lay her hand on his crotch.

Hating himself for his feelings, he became even more irritable. His face went red and he turned away from her. "How many times do I keep telling myself not to get mixed up with you! It always ends up as a circus!" he hissed, his beard trembling with rage.

It wasn't true, it was just that she had hurt him terribly by leaving him, and his perpetually tired wife was bored by her marital duties; he kept vainly hoping to hammer some of Irina's music out of her, but it wasn't there, however hard he shook.

"She's not a woman, she's a bed of nettles," he snorted.

Reb Menashe looked enquiringly at Leva. He knew no Russian, and nothing about Russian emigré life; there were plenty of Russians living in Israel now but no emigrés in Tzfat, where he lived. He was a *sabra,* his mother-tongue was modern Hebrew. He had studied the Judaeo-Islamic culture of the Spanish caliphate, he could read Aramaic, Arabic and Spanish, and he spoke English fluently, with a strong accent. Now he listened to these people's soft speech, and they seemed very pleasant to him.

Nina went over to the two bearded men. Seizing the rabbi's hands in hers, she tossed her shining hair and said to him in Russian: "Thank you for coming. My husband very much wants to talk to you."

Leva translated into Hebrew. The rabbi shook his beard and glanced at Father Victor, who was taking off his surplice.

"It amazes me how quickly the priest gets here in America," he said. "A Jew hasn't even had time to call the rabbi, and he's already arrived."

Father Victor smiled across the room at his colleague from an inimical faith; his benevolence was indiscriminate and unprincipled. When he was younger, he had lived for over a year in Palestine, and he understood Hebrew well enough to give the appropriate response: "I too am one of the guests."

Reb Menashe didn't lift an eyebrow; either he didn't understand or he didn't hear.

Valentina pushed a glass containing a muddy-yellow drink into Father Victor's hand. He sipped carefully.

Out of habit, Reb Menashe averted his eyes from the naked limbs, male and female, just as he did in Tzfat when guffawing foreign tourists piled out of their buses on to the stones of his holy town, repository of the lofty spirit of mystics and kabbalists. He surveyed the people in the room. He had turned away from this life twenty years ago and had never regretted it. His wife Geula was now bearing his tenth child, but had never been naked before him so shamefully as these women here.

"Baruch Ata Adonai . . ." he began the blessing out of habit, giving thanks to the Almighty for having made him a Jew.

"Maybe you'd like something to eat first?" Nina suggested.

Leva raised his hand in a gesture that indicated simultaneously alarm, gratitude and refusal.

Alik lay in the bedroom with his eyes closed. On the inside of his lids, bright yellow and green threads coiled against a flat black background, making rhythmic, intelligible shapes. But although he had studied the ancient language of carpets, he was unable to grasp the basic elements of this moving pattern.

"Alik, you have guests." Nina came in, followed by the rabbi. Lifting his head, she wiped his neck and chest with a wet towel, then pulled the orange sheet off him and waved it over his flat, naked body. Yet again Reb Menashe was startled by this American shamelessness; it was as if they didn't understand the meaning of the word. Out of habit he turned his mind to the place where it was first uttered. Genesis, Chapter Two: "They were both naked and were not ashamed." Who were these children? Why had they no shame? They didn't look sinful, on the contrary they looked innocent. Maybe we had forgotten how to read the Book? Or the Book was written for other people, capable of reading it differently?

Nina raised Alik's legs and joined them at the knees, but they flopped back.

"Leave it, leave it," he said without opening his eyes, looking at the last spiral of the pattern.

Nina pushed a pillow under his knees.

"Thanks, Nina," he replied, and opened his eyes.

A tall thin man in black stood before him with a quizzical look, tilting his head to one side so that the brim of his gleaming black hat almost touched his left shoulder. "Do you speak English, don't you?" he said.

"I do," Alik smiled, winking at Nina.

She went out of the room, followed by Leva.

The rabbi sat on the stool, which was still warm from the priest's buttocks. After hesitating a moment he placed his dusty hat on the edge of Alik's bed, and sat doubled up as though folded in two, his beard falling on to his sharp knees. His huge feet in their worn rubber-soled slip-ons were positioned on the floor with their toes together and heels splayed apart. He was serious, concentrated. His small black skullcap was secured with an invisible hair-clip to his springy dome of greying black hair.

"The thing is, Rabbi, I'm dying," Alik told him.

The rabbi cleared his throat and laced his long fingers together on his knees; he wasn't particularly interested in death.

"You see, my wife's a Christian and wants me to get baptized. To become a Christian." Alik went on, and fell silent. He was becoming less and less keen on this game, and speaking was increasingly difficult for him.

The rabbi too was silent. He stroked his fingers, and finally asked: "So how did this foolishness enter your head?" He hadn't found the correct English word, having meant another kind of foolishness, and added: "Absurdity, I mean."

"Absurd for the ancient Greeks maybe. But for the Jews isn't it a temptation?" The speed of Alik's reactions hadn't deserted him, despite the dull numbness he had almost ceased to feel in his body, but had been feeling for the last few days in his face.

"Should a rabbi know the texts of your apostle then?" Reb Menashe flashed his bright, happy eyes.

"Is there anything a rabbi doesn't know?" Alik parried.

They went on, throwing out questions and not getting answers, as in a Jewish story, understanding each other better perhaps than in reality they should have. They had nothing in common, their upbringing and experiences had been quite different, they ate different food, spoke different languages, read different books. Both were educated people, but the spheres of their education barely intersected. Alik knew nothing of Kalam, the speculative Muslim theology which Reb Menashe had studied for the past twenty years, nor about Saadia Gaon, on whose works he had written his painstaking commentaries; and Reb Menashe knew nothing of Malevich or De Chirico.

"You have no one but the rabbi to seek advice from?" Reb Menashe asked with proud, humorous modesty.

"Can't a Jew seek advice before death from a rabbi?"

In their joking conversation everything was beneath the surface; both understood this, and their banter brought them to the serious point which occurs when people connect, a connection which leaves an indelible trace.

"I feel sorry for my wife, she's crying. What shall I do, Rabbi?" Alik sighed.

The rabbi removed the smile from his face; his moment had come. "Ai-lik!" He wiped the bridge of his nose and shuffled his large shoes. "Ailik! I have lived in Israel practically the whole of my life without leaving it, I'm in America for the first time. I've been here three months and it shocks me. I study philosophy, Jewish philosophy—it's a completely special thing. For a Jew, at the heart of everything is the Torah. If he doesn't study the Torah, he's not a Jew. In ancient times we had this concept of the "captive child." If a Jewish child fell into captivity and was deprived of the Torah, the Jewish way of life, education and upbringing, he was not guilty for this misfortune, nor was he perhaps even capable of understanding it as such. But the Jewish world must take responsibility for the care of these orphans, even those in their advanced years. Here in America I see a whole world consisting entirely of captive children. Millions of Jews living in captivity with the heathens. Never in the history of the Jews has there been anything like it. There have always been apostates, and those who are forcibly baptized—the captive children weren't only in the times of Babylon. But now in the twentieth century there are more captive children than actual Jews. This is a process, and if it's a process, the hand of the Almighty must be there. I think about it all the time, and I'll go on thinking about it for a long time more. You talk about baptism. In other words, go from the category of captive child to that of apostate? But on the other hand you can't be an apostate, because strictly speaking you're not a Jew. The second is worse than the first in my opinion. But then again I may also say that I never had the choice."

How interesting that he had had no choices, Alik thought; I had them till they came out of my arse.

"I was born a Jew," Reb Menashe continued, shaking his thick side locks. "I was a Jew from the beginning and will be one to the end. It's not hard for me. You have the choice. You can be nobody, which I understand to mean a heathen. You could become a Jew, which you have every reason to be by virtue of your blood. Or you can become a Christian, take the crumb that falls from the Jews' table. I won't say if this crumb is good or bad, only that history's source for it has been extremely dubious. If one is honest, isn't the Christian idea of the sacrificing of Christ, understood as a hypostasis of the Almighty, the heathens' greatest victory?"

He chewed his lip and looked quizzically at Alik again. "In my opinion you should at least remain a captive," he concluded. "I assure you, there are some things which are for husbands to decide, not their wives. I can give you no different advice."

Reb Menashe stood up from the uncomfortable stool and suddenly felt dizzy. He craned over Alik from his full height, and began to take his leave: "You are tired, you must rest."

He mumbled some words in a language which Alik didn't understand.

"Wait, Rabbi, I'd like to drink to our leave-taking," he said.

Libin and Rudy carried him into the studio and sat him, or rather arranged him, in his chair.

"He's very weak," thought Father Victor. "How near the miracle is. We should call out to the Lord. Lower him through the roof. God, why are we incapable of that?"

He felt particularly sad, because he knew why.

Leva was in a hurry to take the rabbi away, but Nina came up and offered him a glass.

Leva refused firmly, but the rabbi said something to him.

"Have you paper cups and vodka?" Leva asked Nina.

"Yes, we have," Nina was surprised.

"Fill them up," he said.

Music drifted up from the street like the smell of drains. It was hot too, that New York heat which doesn't diminish at night but raises the energy level towards evening so that many people are troubled by insomnia, especially foreigners, whose bodies carry in them the habits of other climates. This was the case with the rabbi: although accustomed to the heat of Israel, at least the part of it where he had lived in recent years, there the heat of the day would drop, giving people respite from the sun.

Nina brought over two paper cups and handed them to the bearded men.

"After this I'll take you back to the university," Leva said to the rabbi.

"I'm in no hurry," the other replied, thinking of his stuffy room in the hostel, and the long wait for fitful sleep.

Alik sprawled in his chair. Around him were his friends, shouting, laughing and drinking. It was as though he wasn't there, yet they were all focused on him and he felt this. He enjoyed the everydayness of life; like a hunter, he had spent his life chasing after mirages of form and colour, but now he knew there had been nothing better than these senseless parties where people were united by wine, friendship and cheerfulness in this studio with no table, where they laid a makeshift table-top on trestles.

Leva and the rabbi sat in two wobbly easy chairs; in the years when Alik was moving in, the local rubbish-tips had been excellent, and the chairs and the settee were all from there. Opposite Leva and Reb Menashe hung a large painting of Alik's, depicting the Chamber of the Last Supper, with a triple window and a table covered in a white cloth. There were no people seated at the table, just twelve large pomegranates, drawn in meticulous detail in delicate shades of lilac, crimson and pink, rough and full of seeds, their jagged, hypertrophied crowns and vivid dents evoking their internal partitioned structure. Beyond the triple window lay the Holy Land, seen as it is now rather than in the imagination of Leonardo da Vinci.

Reb Menashe was not a connoisseur of art. He stared at the painting, and at first he saw only the bright-red fruits; it was an old debate precisely which fruit had tempted Khava, the apple, the pomegranate or the peach. The room portrayed in the painting was also familiar to him: the so-called Chamber of the Last Supper was situated directly on top of the tomb of David in the Old City.

"All the same, the picture speaks of a purely Jewish chastity," he decided, looking at it. "He has replaced the people with pomegranates, that's his trick, poor man."

Reb Menashe had been born two days after the declaration of the state of Israel. His grandfather was a Zionist who had organized one of the first agricultural colonies. His father had lived for the underground army, the Hagana. The rabbi himself had both fought and dug the land. He was born under the walls of the Old City, by the Windmill of Montefiore, and the first view he remembered seeing from the window was of the Gates of Zion.

He was twenty when he followed the tanks and entered these gates for the first time. The Old City still smelt of fire and metal. He had scrambled through it, exploring its maze of Arab streets, the roofs of the Christian and Armenian quarters. The Christian holy places of Jerusalem seemed dubious to him, as did many of the Judaic ones. The Chamber of the Last Supper aroused his particular mistrust: it seemed highly unlikely that this secret paschal meeting would have been organized over the bones of the Great King. But David's tomb itself raised serious doubts. This astonishing world which he so loved, of weak white stone, fluctuating light and hot air, was filled with historical and archaeological implausibilities, unlike the world of bookish wisdom, which was organized with crystal clarity, without approximations or anomalies, rising intelligibly upward with paradoxically logical convolutions of great beauty.

He had understood for the first time what this land meant for him when he left it. He was young then; he had graduated from university and had been sent to Germany to study philosophy. A year of concentrated study exhausted his interest in European philosophy, torn off from its living roots, which he recognized exclusively in the Torah. This ended the brief period of his academic education, and in the second half of his third decade, he embarked on the traditional path of Judaic science which is more accurately called theology.

He had married a silent girl who shaved off her vibrant auburn tresses the day before the wedding, and since then he had enjoyed the harmony which comes from a life whose every detail is regulated with clockwork precision, and from the intellectual rigours of being at the same time both teacher and pupil.

His world had completely changed: the information which most people receive from radio, television and the secular press passed him by, and he was nourished by the ancient code of Shulkhan Arukh, the table laid for those who wish to partake of the Jewish spiritual heritage, and by the high-voiced clamour of his many children.

Five years later his first book was published, an exploration of the stylistic differences between Saadia's commentaries on Daniel and the Chronicles. Two years after this he moved to Tzfat.

His world was biblically simple and talmudically complicated, yet all its facets connected, and his daily work with his medieval texts cast a shadow of the eternal over the present. Below him at the bottom of the mountain shone the blue Sea of Galilee, and he experienced a deep feeling of gratitude to the Almighty—Christians might call it Phariseeism—for the happy fate that had been granted to him of serving and knowing, and for the holiness of this land which appears to many as a dirty, provincial eastern state, but which for him was the undisputed centre of the world, in relation to which all other states with their histories and cultures could be read only as commentaries.

The priest had already removed his surplice and was pushing through the crowd of guests towards him. "I hear you've come from Israel to teach a course of Judaics?" he asked in school-book English.

Reb Menashe stood up. He had never talked to a priest

before. "Yes, I'm lecturing on Judaeo-Islamic culture at the Jewish university here."

"They do some wonderful courses, I once read a book about biblical archaeology published by that university." The priest broke into a happy smile. "Your Judaeo-Islamic theme is presumably developed in the context of the contemporary world by some sort of trade-off?"

"Trade-off?" Reb Menashe didn't understand the expression. "No no, political parallels don't concern me, I'm interested in philosophy." He seemed agitated.

Alik called to Valentina. "Valentina, keep an eye on those two and make sure they don't stay sober!"

Valentina came over, pink and plump, holding more paper cups to her chest. She put them before Leva, and the three men drank together. A moment later their heads came together, they nodded their beards and gesticulated. Alik looked at them with deep satisfaction and said to Libin: "I think I've successfully played the role of Saladin today."

Valentina sought Libin's eyes and nodded towards the kitchen. A moment later she was squeezing him into a corner. "I can't ask her, you'll have to," she said urgently.

"I see, you can't, so it's down to me." Libin was offended.

"That's enough. We must pay right now, at least for one month!"

"We've only just been asking for money."

"Just—a month ago," Valentina shrugged. "Why should I fork out more than anyone else? I paid the phone bill last month, it was all out-of-town calls. Nina talks a lot when she's drinking."

"She's only just given money," Libin sighed.

"Okay, ask someone else then, how about Faika?"

Libin burst out laughing: Faika was up to her ears in debt, and there wasn't a person in this room to whom she didn't owe at least ten dollars. Libin had no choice but to go to Irina.

Money wasn't just a mess, it was a disaster. In the years before Alik became ill he had sold few paintings, and now that he had stopped working and could no longer run around the galleries his income was virtually zero, or rather less than zero. Debts grew: those which had to be settled, such as rent and phone bills, and those which would never be paid, like medical bills.

As well as this there was another unpleasant story, which had dragged on for several years. Two gallery-owners from Washington had organized an exhibition for Alik and had failed to return twelve of his works. Alik himself was partly to blame for this, and it would never have happened if he had gone back to the gallery on the day the exhibition closed, as they had agreed, and taken everything back. But he was enjoying in advance the sale of three of his paintings, and had borrowed the money to go off to Jamaica with Nina, so he didn't make the final day. Even when he came back he didn't go immediately. The cheque for the paintings didn't arrive for some reason, so he phoned Washington to find out why. They asked him where he had been, and told him the works had been returned and had had to be put in storage, since the gallery had no space for them. This was a barefaced lie.

Alik had asked Irina to help. Another fact emerged: when he signed the contract he had left his copy with the gallery-owners. This blunder gave them the upper hand and made them even more brazen, and there seemed to be almost nothing Irina could do about it. All she had was the catalogue of the exhibition, which contained information about the paintings and a reproduction of one of those that had ostensibly been sold. She embarked on the process of suing the gallery, and while the case creaked on she reluctantly made Alik out a cheque for five thousand dollars. She told him she had screwed it out of them; in reality she still was fairly hopeful of recovering some of the money.

It was the beginning of winter. When she gave Alik the cheque he was overjoyed: "I'm lost for words, I can't thank you enough, now we can pay the rent and finally buy Nina that fur coat."

Irina was furious; she hadn't given him money she had earned by the sweat of her brow to buy fur coats. But there was nothing to be done, half of the money was blown on a coat. Nina and Alik were like that; they never did anything by halves.

"Bloody bohemians," Irina fumed. "Perhaps they haven't eaten enough shit since they've been here."

Exhaling the hot breath from her lungs, she decided that she would help them in future with small sums, in response to their immediate needs. She was a single woman with a child after all, and not nearly as rich as they seemed to think she was; it was hard enough for her to earn the damned stuff in the first place.

When Libin came up to her she already had her cheque-book out. Over time the small sums grew unnoticed, like children.

NINE

The bearded men walked out to the street. Gottlieb didn't feel drunk at all, but he had forgotten where he had left his car, and the place where he expected to find it was occupied by someone else's long-backed Pontiac.

"They've towed it away, they've towed it away!" Father Victor laughed like a child, without malice.

"You can park here, why would they tow it away?" Gottlieb said peevishly. "You wait, I'll look round the corner."

The rabbi displayed no interest in which car they would be driving him back in, he was more intrigued by what the funny man in the cap was saying: "With your permission, I'd like to go on," Father Victor was in a hurry to share his thoughts with his unusual companion. "The first experiment was successful, you might say. The diaspora proved exceptionally valuable for the entire world. Of course you've brought back together what's left of you over there, but so many Jews have assimilated, diluted, there are so many of you in all countries, in science, culture, the arts. In some ways I'm a Judophile. Every decent Christian must respect the chosen people. You understand how important it is that Jews have poured their precious blood into every culture, every nation. And from this what do we get? It's a worldwide process! The Russians leave their ghetto, and the Chinese. Mark my words, from these young American Chinese we're getting the best musicians, the best mathematicians. I'll go further—mixed marriages! You see what I'm saying? It's the creating of a new people!"

The rabbi appeared to understand quite well what his opponent was saying, but he didn't by any means share his thoughts on the subject and merely chewed his lip. Three glasses or four. He couldn't remember, at any event it had evidently been a lot.

"We're living in new times! Neither Jew nor gentile, and in the most direct sense too!" the priest said happily.

The rabbi stopped walking and wagged a finger at him. "That's it, that's the most important thing for you isn't it—no Jews."

Gottlieb finally drove up in his car, opened the door for his rabbi, then rudely drove off leaving Father Victor alone on the street in a state of deep mortification. "Look how he twists things, I meant nothing of the sort."

TEN

~People didn't so much disperse as melt away. A few stayed behind to sleep on the carpet. One of those on the carpet that night was Nina; this night was Valentina's.

Alik fell asleep as soon as the guests left, and Valentina curled up at his feet. She could have slept there, but as though to spite her, sleep didn't come; she had noticed that alcohol had lately had the strange effect of driving it out.

She had arrived in New York in November 1981. She was twenty-eight, 165 centimetres tall, and weighed 85 kilograms. She didn't reckon in pounds then. She was wearing a black hand-woven wool-embroidered shirt from the Gutsul region of the Ukraine. In her cheap cloth suitcase she carried her completed dissertation, of no possible use to her now, a complete holiday costume as worn by a Vologda peasant woman from the late nineteenth century, and three Antonov apples which she was forbidden to import, and whose powerful smell emanated from her feeble case. The apples were intended for her American husband, who for some reason wasn't there to meet her.

A week earlier she had bought her ticket for New York and had called to tell him she was coming. He seemed happy and promised to meet her. Their marriage was a fictitious one, but they were true friends. Mickey had lived for a year in Russia, collecting material on the Soviet cinema of the thirties and enduring a neurasthenic love affair with a little monster who humiliated and robbed him and put him through a hell of jealousy. He had met Valentina at Moscow's fashionable philology school. She had taken him back to her place, given him valerian drops to drink, fed him Russian dumplings and finally heard the shattering confession of a homosexual crushed by the incontrovertibility of his own nature. Mickey was tall and delicate-looking. He wept and poured out his anguish to her, keeping up a running psychoanalytical commentary all the while. Her heart melted, and she marvelled at the capriciousness of nature. During a brief respite in his two-hour monologue she asked him: "So you've never been with a woman then?"

It proved not quite so simple: when he was fourteen, his seventeen-year-old cousin from Connecticut had stayed in their house for a month and a half and had tormented him with her caresses, finally abandoning him in a state of exhausting virginity and indelible sinfulness.

This emotional tale, crammed with relevant details, seemed a little too literary to Valentina, and by the time it was over she was exhausted. Laying his hands firmly on her fine nipples, she raped him without any great difficulty and to his complete satisfaction. It remained the only such occasion in his life, but from then on their relationship assumed an unusual warmth and intimacy.

Valentina was experiencing her own emotional crisis at the time, having just been stunningly betrayed by the man she loved. He was a well-known dissident who had survived a stint in prison, and was widely regarded as a hero of irreproachable honesty and courage. But there was evidently a joint running between his upper and lower halves: the upper half was exemplary, the lower was vicious. With women he was insatiable and promiscuous, and he used all of them. His departure from Russia was mourned by many beautiful girlfriends of the most extreme anti-Soviet persuasion, and the lives of at least two illegitimate children would have to be sustained only by heroic legends about their father.

He had married an Italian beauty and left Russia in a blaze of glory, abandoning Valentina with her KGB "tail" and her unsubmitted dissertation. Big-hearted Mickey proposed a fictitious liaison, so they got married. For decorum's sake they held the wedding in Kaluga, where Valentina's mother lived, and from that day on she was reconciled with her daughter. She didn't like her husband and referred to him privately as "the tapeworm." But his American passport worked its charm even on her; at the print-works where she had worked all her life as a cleaner, no one had yet married their daughter to an American.

After waiting two hours for her husband at Kennedy airport, Valentina finally called his home. There was no answer, so she decided to go to the address he had given her. She asked some friendly Americans the way, and they explained that the place wasn't in New York at all but in the suburbs. (She had picked up a few bits and pieces of English but they didn't amount to much.) More or less knowing what she was doing, she set off for the address she had written down.

A sense of the complete unreality of what was happening freed her from normal human anxieties. However the future worked out, it was bound to be better than the past: behind her everything was cursed.

With these happy thoughts she boarded the bus. For some reason nobody took her money. She wondered if this was what the "land of the free" meant and was glad she didn't have to pay; she had fifty dollars on her, and she would have to hold on to them if she was to track down her errant husband.

The sun was setting when after several small adventures and large impressions she got out at Tarrytown. She breathed in the evening air and sat down on a yellow bench at the bus station. She hadn't slept for over thirty-six hours, everything was moving about in front of her eyes and her head was spinning from a sense of weightlessness and uncertainty.

After sitting there for ten minutes she picked up her case, walked out into a little square lined with parked cars, and asked a young man fiddling with the lock of his vehicle how to find the street she wanted. Without saying a word, he flung open the passenger door and drove her up a hill to a pretty two-storey house surrounded by well-tended shrubs. The light was fading. She stopped in front of a pair of white slatted gates.

Rachel, Mickey's mother, had been bothered all morning by a wonderful dream she had had before waking. In it she had come upon a white wooden summer-house which didn't exist in their garden, where a sweet, plump little girl had talked to her about something very important and pleasant, even though she was only tiny and in real life small children don't talk like that. What she had said, however, Rachel couldn't remember.

During the day she had lain down for a nap and tried to summon back the airy summer-house and the plump child, so that she could finish the important matter she had been talking about. But the little girl didn't reappear, and there was no point expecting her to, since Rachel never dreamed during the day.

Now she waddled to the gates, a simple-faced Jewish woman with round eyes ringed by years of insomnia, and she saw a girl standing outside with a checked cloth suitcase. She let her in.

"Good evening, may I speak to Mickey?" the girl asked.

"Mickey?" Rachel was surprised. "He doesn't live here, he lives in Manhattan. He left for California yesterday anyway."

Valentina put her case on the ground. "How strange, he said he would meet me."

"Ah, that's Mickey!" Rachel waved an arm. "Where are you from?"

"From Moscow."

As Valentina stood against the white gates, Rachel suddenly realized that the summer-house in her dream must be these gates, and that the plump child was this plump girl. "My God, my parents were from Warsaw!" she exclaimed happily, as though Warsaw and Moscow were adjacent streets. "Come on in!"

A few minutes later Valentina was sitting at a low table in the living-room, looking out at a sloping garden whose trees bent their heads in the gathering darkness towards the brightly lit window. On the table stood two delicate unglazed cups as thin as paper, and a rough terracotta teapot; there were biscuits that resembled seaweed, and pink triangular nuts with a fine shell. Rachel put her hands on her stomach in the same peasant pose as Valentina's mother, tilted her head in its green silk turban to one side, and looked at her with kindly interest. It turned out that the Russian woman knew Polish, so they talked in Polish together, which gave Rachel great satisfaction.

"You've come here on holiday or to work?" she finally put the all-important question.

"I've come for good. Mickey promised to meet me and help me find work," Valentina sighed.

"You met him in Moscow?" Rachel asked, tipping her head to the other shoulder: she had this funny habit of tilting her head from side to side.

Valentina thought hard for a moment; she was so tired that having a worldly conversation in Polish, let alone embellishing it a little, suddenly seemed beyond her strength. "The truth is, we got married."

The blood rushed to Rachel's face. Jumping up, she ran out of the room. "David, David! Come quick!" her voice rang through the house.

David, her husband, tall and thin like Mickey, stood at the top of the stairs in a red shirt and black skullcap, holding a thick fountain-pen in his hand, peering at her with a questioning look but saying nothing.

They were a fine pair, Mickey's parents. Each discovered in the other what they lacked in themselves, and they rejoiced at the discovery. Several years ago, having reached the limits of human closeness, they were approaching their sixties and looking forward to a long and happy old age, when they learned to their horror that their only son had turned away from the laws of his sex and had deviated into such heathen wickedness that Rachel couldn't even find a name for it.

"We were happy, too happy," she muttered through the sleepless nights in the huge marriage bed in which they hadn't touched each other since their terrible discovery. "Lord, make him a normal person again!"

The popular psychology books explained to her in clear and simple words that there was nothing unusual about her son, everything was fine, and a humane society must grant him his sacred and inalienable right to his own predilections. But this was no comfort to Rachel's old-fashioned soul. A Jewish girl, saved from the fire and gas by the nuns, who for almost three years during the occupation had hidden her in their convent, she reached the point of turning to the mother of that God in whom she mustn't believe, but did believe nonetheless, and praying to her in Polish: "Holy Mother, do this for him, make him . . ."

As her husband came down the stairs to her now and saw her happy face, he guessed the happiness that had befallen her.

But this happiness was fictitious: Valentina was sitting in the living-room struggling to keep her tired eyes open. This was how her life in America began.

Alik stirred slightly.

Valentina started up. "What is it, Alik?"

"Drink."

She brought the cup to his lips. He sipped and coughed. She lifted him up and tapped his back; he was as light as the puppet Anka Kron had given him. "There now, let's get your tube."

He took more water into his mouth and coughed again. This had been happening a lot recently. Valentina moved him again and tapped his back. She gave him the tube, and again he coughed, longer this time, and couldn't clear his throat. She wet a flannel and put it in his mouth. His lips were dry and slightly cracked.

"Shall I rub something on your lips?" she asked.

"On no account, I hate grease. Give me your finger instead."

She put her finger between his dry lips and he moved his tongue over it. It was the only touch left to him now; it looked as though this would be the last night they made love. They both thought about it.

"I shall die an adulterer," he said quietly.

Valentina's life had been exceptionally difficult in those early years. She generally went straight from work to her classes. But one day she had had to go home early after her landlady called asking her to bring the keys because something was wrong with the front door, Valentina didn't understand exactly what. She gave the landlady her key, but this didn't work either. Leaving the landlady with the broken lock, she decided to get something to eat at Katz's, the Jewish delicatessen on the corner, before she went on to her class. The prices at Katz's were reasonable, and the corned beef and turkey sandwiches were superb. The burly staff, who looked as if they could handle concrete slabs, sliced the fragrant meat artistically with their large knives and chatted in their local dialect. The place was rather full, and there was a queue at the counter. The man standing in front of Valentina with his back to her spoke affably to the salesman: "Listen, Misha, ten years I've been coming here. You and Aron, you're twice as fat and the sandwiches are half as thick. Why is that?"

Flashing his bare hands, Aron winked at Valentina: "You think he's dropping me a hint?"

The man in front of Valentina turned to look at her. He had a stiff red pony-tail tied in a rubber band, his freckled face was laughing, his red moustache bristled cheerfully. "He thinks it's a hint. It's not a hint, it's the riddle of life!"

Misha speared a gherkin on to a fork, then another, and laid them beside the succulent sandwich on a cardboard plate. "Here's an extra pickle for you, Alik." He turned to Valentina. "He says he's an artist but I know he's from the consumer rights department back home. They follow me even here. You want pastrami?"

Valentina nodded. Misha flashed his knife. The man with the red moustache sat down at a nearby table where another place had become free and took Valentina's paper plate from her hands, putting it on the table and pushing a chair back for her with his foot. She sat down silently.

"You're from Moscow?" he said.

She nodded.

"Been here long?"

"A month and a half."

"I thought so, you haven't the seasoned look yet." His expression was direct and good-natured. "What do you do?"

"Babysitting, classes, you know."

"Excellent!" he said. "You've found your feet quickly."

Valentina pulled apart the two halves of her sandwich.

"No, no! What are you doing? No one eats like that! Americans won't stand for it, it's sacred! Just open your mouth wide and make sure you don't spill the ketchup." He bit neatly around the bulging edge of his sandwich. "Life's very simple here. They don't have many rules, but you have to know what they are."

"Rules?" asked Valentina, obediently putting back the two halves of her sandwich.

"That's the first one. The second is to smile." He smiled at her with his mouth full of sandwich.

"And the third?"

"What's your name?"

"Valentina."

"Mm," he murmured, "Valechka."

"Valentina," she corrected him. She had always hated the name Valechka, ever since childhood.

"Right, Valentina, maybe we don't know each other that well yet, but never mind, I'll tell you. The second Newtonian law formulates itself thus: smile, but cover your arse."

Valentina laughed, and ketchup dripped onto her scarf.

"Then of course there's the third," Alik went on, wiping the ketchup off. "Start with the first two. These are the best sandwiches in America. That's right, this eating-place is almost a hundred years old. Edgar Allan Poe came here—Jack London, O. Henry, they all bought sandwiches at this place for a dime. Americans don't know these writers, by the way. Well, maybe they teach Poe in school. But if the owner here had read just one of them, he'd hang his portrait on the wall. That's our American misfortune, our sandwiches are fine but there's not enough culture. Although you can bet that the grandson of the first Katz graduated from Harvard—I don't mean Adam but the first owner—and that his grandson studied in Paris at the

Sorbonne and probably took part in the student revolution of
1968 . . ."

Valentina didn't have the courage to ask which revolution he had in mind, but Alik put his sandwich down and went
on: "The gherkins are pickled in the barrel, you don't find ones
like these anywhere else. They pickle them themselves. To be
honest, I like them softer and more shrivelled, but they aren't
bad, at least they don't use vinegar. This is a stunning city, it's
got everything. The city of cities, the Tower of Babel! But it's
worth it, my God it's worth it!" He seemed not to be speaking
to her, but arguing with someone who wasn't there.

"But it's so dirty and depressing and there are so many
black people here," Valentina said softly.

"You come from Russia, and you think America's dirty?
That's a good one! And the black people, they're New York's
finest decoration! You don't like music? What's America without music! And it's black music, black music!" He was hurt
and angry. "You know nothing at all about it, so you'd better
shut up!"

They finished eating and went outside. At the door of the
café he asked, "Where are you going?"

"To Washington Square, I'm doing classes there."

"English?"

She nodded. "Advanced."

"I'll walk you there. I live just a few blocks away. Go up
to Astor Place and turn the corner," he waved an arm, "that's
where the punks hang out. They're amazing, all in black
leather and way-out metal. American punks have nothing in
common with the English ones, and their music is something
else too. Near the square is the old Ukrainian quarter—it's not
that interesting. Oh, and there's an amazing Irish pub, a real
one. They don't even let women in. Well, they probably do

now, but there are no ladies' toilets, only urinals. This isn't a city, it's a huge living street theatre. For years I haven't been able to tear myself away from it."

They walked through the Bowery. He stopped her by one of the grey, gloomy buildings which seemed to fill this neighbourhood. "Look, that's CBGB, the most important place for music in the world. In a hundred years people will hoard scraps of plaster from these walls in gold boxes. I mean it. A new culture is being born here. The Knitting Factory is the same. Geniuses play here every night."

A skinny black boy in a pink-and-white coat jumped out of a peeling doorway. Alik greeted him.

"What did I tell you? That's Booby the flute player. Every evening he plays with God. I've just been here buying tickets for his concert. My wife won't come with me, she doesn't like this kind of music. Would you come with me?"

"I can only manage Sundays," Valentina replied. "Every other day I'm busy from eight in the morning until eleven at night."

"I see, hard to get," Alik grinned.

"Well, that's how it is—I'm at work by nine, I finish at six, at seven I have classes, then next day I babysit my land-lady's granddaughter. At eleven I'm free, at twelve I go to sleep. Three hours later I wake up, and that's it. I have this American insomnia, God knows what it is. At three in the morning I'm like one of those dolls that never falls over. I've tried going to bed later but it makes no difference, after three I can't get back to sleep."

"Well, there are no concerts at that time, but there are plenty of places where things go on till morning. It doesn't matter when we go, three's okay."

Nina was a serious alcoholic by then and her needs were

very simple. During the day she drank half a bottle of Russian vodka diluted with American juice, by one in the morning she was sleeping the sleep of the just. Alik would carry her from the armchair to the bedroom and would sleep beside her for a few hours. He was one of those people who don't need much sleep, like Napoleon.

Alik's affair with Valentina was conducted between the hours of three and eight. It didn't start at once but gradually. Two months passed before he finally entered the basement room which Rachel had found for her in the house of one of her friends.

For the first two months he would visit twice a week at three in the morning. Stooping, he would whistle down to her dimly lit window. Ten minutes later she would hop out, pink and healthy in her black Gutsul shirt, and they would go to one of those night places which were rarely frequented by emigrés.

During one of the coldest nights of January, when the snow had lain on the ground for almost the whole week, they ended up at the fish market. Two steps from Wall Street teemed the most incredible life. Ships docked at the harbour from all over the world, and fishermen would hump their live, or, on this occasion, frozen wares on their backs, on carts and in baskets. The wide doors in the walls of the warehouses burst open to receive these marine riches. Two solidly built men bore on their shoulders a miraculous log of silver tuna, covered in a thin film of ice. On the stalls were arranged ordinary, unexceptional little mongrel fish, but the eye was drawn to the profusion of amazing sea monsters, with terrible eyes, claws and suckers. There were fish which seemed to consist entirely of mouths, and a large number of fantastic-looking shellfish, with their thin slivers of meat inside. There were snake-like animals with sweet faces that reminded one of mermaids; there were intermediate life-forms, part animal, part plant; and there was unambiguous seaweed, layered and trailing like vines. In the white light of the lamps the colours merged in a swirl of blue, red, green and pink. Some creatures still stirred, some had already stiffened.

In the alleyways stood several iron braziers with flames licking from them, and from time to time freezing people would hurry over to warm themselves there. The people here were as marvellous as their wares: Norwegians with auburn beards streaked by hoar-frost, whiskered Chinese, island people with ancient, exotic faces. Pushing through them were wholesalers from all over New York and New Jersey drawn by the low prices, as well as cooks and owners of the best restaurants, drawn by the fresh goods.

"It's like a fairy-story!" Valentina laughed, and Alik was happy to have found someone who was as crazy about it as he was.

"What did I tell you?" He pulled her into a café to drink whiskey, because it was essential to drink in this freezing weather. The owner greeted him, of course.

"He's my friend. Look over here," he jabbed a finger at the wall, where beside the prints of yachts and ships and the photos of people Valentina didn't know hung a small painting depicting two insignificant fish: a reddish one with a spiky, wide-open fin, a greyish one like a herring. "For that picture Robert said I could drink on the house for the rest of my life."

Sure enough, the bald, red-faced patron was already handing them two whiskies.

There was a large crowd of sailors, loaders and traders here. It was a man's place, with no women present. The men drank and ate the café's fish soup, but the food wasn't the point. They came not to eat but to drink, rest and get warm. The cold was exceptional for New Yorkers; they didn't seem to understand, the way true northerners do, that you don't keep warm by putting on a fur coat over a thin shirt, stuffing two pairs of nylon socks inside rubber boots and sticking a baseball cap on your head.

"Drink up quick, or we'll miss the best bit," Alik hurried Valentina up.

They went out to the street again. During the half-hour they had been inside, everything had changed at cartoon speed. The stalls had been cleared away, the doors of the warehouses had closed and turned back into solid walls, the braziers with the cheerful flames had gone, and a posse of tall lads walked down from the direction of the harbour hosing the scraps of fish off the ground. Fifteen minutes later Alik and Valentina stood almost alone on this promontory on the southernmost tip of Manhattan, and the whole night spectacle seemed like a dream.

"Okay, let's go and drink some more," Alik said. He took her to a diner empty of people. The tables sparkled with cleanliness. A young boy, the owner's son, had just finished mopping the floor. He too nodded at Alik.

"This isn't all either. In exactly fifteen minutes we'll see the final act."

In exactly fifteen minutes the nearby subway spewed out a crowd of elegantly dressed men and coiffed women, wearing good shoes, smart suits and this season's perfumes.

"Mother of God, where are they off to, a party?" Valentina gasped.

"They're clerks and secretaries mostly, they work in Wall Street. A lot of them live in Hoboken, another fascinating place I'll show you one day. They're not that rich, they make about sixty to a hundred thousand a year. White-collar workers, the most slavish breed."

They walked to the station, because it was time for Valentina to go to work. She looked around, but where the fish market had been there was just a faint smell of fish, which you had to sniff hard to catch.

As well as the fish market were the meat and flower markets. In the flower market you could get lost among the tubs with trees; it opened at night and went on throughout the day. Outside the meat market they once met a red-haired man with a familiar face. Alik exchanged a couple of words with him, then they walked on.

"Who was that?"

"Didn't you recognize him? That was Brodsky, he lives near here."

"The living Brodsky?" Valentina asked in surprise.

It truly was the living Brodsky.

They also visited a dance club, with a unique clientele of rich elderly ladies and decrepit gentlemen, mothballed lovers of the tango, the foxtrot and the Boston waltz.

Sometimes they just walked. Then one night they kissed, and after that they almost stopped walking. Alik would whistle from the street, and Valentina would open the door.

For a while Valentina moved into Mickey's apartment after he left to teach for several years at a well-known film school in California. His personal life changed for the better, although Rachel still grieved that instead of sweet, plump Valentina whose large breasts could have fed as many grandchildren as you could wish for, Mickey's lover was a little Spanish professor who specialized in the works of García Lorca.

Mickey's apartment was downtown, and Alik would visit Valentina there, still between the sacred hours of three and eight.

There was a time when she refused his visits. She had moved to Queens, where she had been hired by the college there to teach Russian. In Queens she had another man, also from Russia; no one had seen him, they only knew that he worked as a truck-driver. It was unclear how long the truck-driver lasted in Valentina's life, but when after stiff competition she got a proper American job teaching in one of the New York universities, he was no longer on the scene and Alik was back again. This time she knew it was for ever, and that no one would leave anyone, neither Valentina Alik, nor Alik Nina.

ELEVEN

Lyuda, an engineer from Moscow, had been brought to the apartment the day before, had spent the night on the carpet and stayed. In the morning, the quietest time of the day, when those with jobs had left, those on benefits hadn't opened their eyes, and Nina hadn't shaken off her orange-juice dream, this unprepossessing, unmemorable woman washed yesterday's cups and glasses then looked in on Alik. He was already awake.

"I'm Lyuda, from Moscow," she repeated to be on the safe side; she had been introduced to him yesterday, but she was used to people not remembering her name.

"A long time?" Alik was instantly awake.

"Six days. It seems like a long time. Shall I wash you?" She asked this lightly as though her main activity were to wash the sick every morning. She took a wet towel and wiped his face, neck and hands.

"So what's new in Moscow?" Alik asked mechanically.

"Nothing changes. Twaddle on the radio, the shops are empty, what's new. You want breakfast?"

"Well, let's try."

Eating was difficult for him. For the last two weeks he had eaten only baby food, and he had trouble getting even this fruity mush down him.

"I'll make you some potato puree." Lyuda was already in the kitchen, rattling plates and saucepans.

The puree was thin and slipped down easily. Alik felt better this morning: the light wasn't so blurred, and his vision was clearer and didn't play tricks on him.

Lyuda plumped up his pillows, and thought sadly that it seemed to be her fate to bury everyone. In forty-five years she had buried her mother, her father, two grandmothers, her grandfather, her first husband, and only recently a close girl-friend. She fed them and washed them all, then she washed their bodies. This one wasn't even hers, someone had brought her to him.

She had a mass of things to do, a long list of items to buy and strangers to visit, people who wanted to question her about their Moscow relatives and tell her about their lives, but she already felt part of this ridiculous household; it was as if she couldn't tear herself away from this man she was beginning to love, and her heart would break again in exactly the same place.

The telephone rang. She picked it up, and someone shouted down the line: "Turn on CNN! There's a coup in Moscow!"

"There's a coup in Moscow," Lyuda said in a faltering voice. "That's something new for you."

Scattered fragments of a news bulletin flashed across the television screen. Some kind of civil emergency, ugly thuggish faces, thick-voiced, with corruption written all over them, like ill-fitting false teeth.

"Where do they find these ugly mugs?" Alik wondered aloud.

"And the ones here are any better?" Lyuda burst out with unexpected patriotism.

"Yes they are," Alik thought a little. "Of course they're better. They're all crooks here too of course, but at least they're ashamed. Those ones have no shame."

It was impossible to make sense of what was happening. Gorbachev apparently had a health problem.

"They've probably killed him by now," Alik said.

The telephone rang incessantly. An event like this was impossible to keep to oneself.

Lyuda moved the television to make it easier for Alik to see.

Her ticket was for 6 September. She must change it immediately and go back. Go back to what, though? Her son was here, her husband would do better to join them. But what could they do here, without the language, without anything? At home they had their books and their friends, a thousand dear people. Now all of them were swept up in this transient cloud on the screen.

"I said something would happen before that treaty was signed," said Alik with satisfaction.

"What treaty?" said Lyuda, who didn't follow politics because they repelled her.

"Wake Nina up," Alik begged her.

But Nina was already creeping into the bedroom.

"Mark my words, everything is being decided now," said Alik prophetically.

"What's being decided?" Nina was flustered and still half-asleep; all events outside the apartment were equally remote to her.

By evening a mass of people had gathered again. The television was carried from the bedroom and put on the floor of the studio, and everyone surged away from Alik and crowded around it. Something incomprehensible was happening: a twitching marionette popped up, a bathhouse superintendent, a moustached man with a face like a dog, half-devils, half-people, phantasmagoria from the dream sequence in *Evgeny Onegin*, and the tanks. Troops were entering Moscow. Huge tanks were sliding through the streets of the city, and it was unclear who was fighting whom.

Lyuda clutched her temples and groaned: "What's happening? What will happen next?"

Her son, a young computer-programmer, had got off early from work and was sitting next to her a little embarrassed. "What will happen? There'll be a military dictatorship of course."

They tried to get through to Moscow, but all the lines were busy. No doubt tens of thousands of people were dialling Moscow numbers all at the same time.

"Look, look, the tanks are passing our building!"

The tanks were moving down the Garden ring road now.

"What are you crying about? Your son's here, you'll stay and that's that," Faika tried to console Lyuda.

"Father probably retired long ago," Nina said irrelevantly.

Only Alik understood the relevance of this remark:

Nina's father was a dedicated, high-ranking KGB man who had renounced her when she left Russia, and had forbidden her mother to write to her.

"To hell with it, the regime's a bitch and all the vodka's gone!" Libin jumped up and ran to the lift.

Gioia, who read Russian quite well but whose understanding of the spoken language was poor, suddenly found her ears opening in these hours and each word spoken by the announcer she caught on the wing. She was one of those people who, without ever visiting it, fall in love with a foreign country and know it from old books, and in bad translations at that. Now, by some unexpected inspiration, she understood everything in the announcer's script. Rudy the painter gawped at the screen and fidgeted, tugging at her elbow and demanding a translation.

What was going on in Moscow was so hard to understand that it seemed as if everyone needed a translation.

People forgot about Alik for a while, and he closed his eyes. The events on the screen moved before him like flashing spots. By evening he was tired, but his mind was still clear.

Maika sat beside him on the arm of the easy chair, and stroked his shoulder. "Will there be a war in Russia?" she asked him quietly.

"War? I don't think so. Unhappy country."

Maika wrinkled her forehead. "I've already heard that. Poor, rich, developed, backward, okay. But unhappy country? I don't get it."

"You're clever, Teeshirt, you know that?" Alik looked at her with astonishment and satisfaction, and that she understood.

All the people sitting here who had been born in Russia differed in their gifts, their education and human qualities, but they were united by the single act of leaving it. The majority had emigrated legally, some were non-returnees, the most audacious of them ran away across the borders. Yet however their life in emigration had worked out, however much their views differed, they had this one thing in common: this crossed frontier, this crossed, stumbling lifeline, this tearing up of old roots and putting down of new ones in new earth, with its new colours, smells and structures.

As the years went by, even their bodies changed their composition: the molecules of the New World entered their blood and replaced everything old from home. Their reactions, their behaviour and their way of thinking gradually altered, but the one thing they still needed was some proof of the correctness of what they had done. The more complicated and insurmountable the difficulties they faced in America, the more necessary this proof was for them. Consciously or not, the news from Moscow about the growing stupidity, lack of talent and criminality of life there during these years provided the proof they needed. But none could have imagined that what was happening in that far-off place which they had all but erased from their lives would be so painful for them now. It turned out that this country sat in their souls, their guts, and that whatever they thought about it—and they all thought different things—their links with it were unbreakable. It was like some chemical reaction in the blood, something nauseating, bitter and terrible.

For a long time Russia had existed for them only in their

dreams. They all dreamed the same dream, but with different variations. Alik had once collected and recorded these dreams in an exercise-book which he called "An Emigré's Dreambook." The basic structure of the dream was as follows: they arrived back to find themselves in a closed building, or a building without doors, or a rubbish-container; or something happened that made it impossible for them to return to America: losing documents or being sent to prison, for instance; one Jew had even seen his dead mother, who had tied him up with a rope.

Alik had had an amusing variant of the dream. He was back in Moscow, everything was bright and beautiful, and his old friends were celebrating his return in a large flat, which was familiar yet dreadfully neglected. This friendly scrum of people then accompanied him to Sheremetevo airport, but it was nothing like the heart-rending farewells of past years when everything was for ever, until death. When the time came for him to board the plane, his old friend Sasha Nolikov suddenly appeared and pushed some dogs' leads into his hand. On the end of them a pack of variously coloured little mongrels jumped about, with husky blood in their veins and with curly tails like pretzels. Sasha disappeared and all of Alik's friends departed, leaving him alone with the dogs. There was nobody he could give them to, and the check-in for New York was already closing. Then an airline official came to tell him the plane was in the air, and he stayed with the dogs in Moscow knowing that this was for ever. He worried only about how Nina would pay the rent on their Manhattan studio, and in his dream he could smell the lift, the loft, the unavoidable odour of rough tobacco . . .

"Tell me, Alik, was life so bad there?" Maika again touched his shoulder.

"Silly, we had an excellent life. But life's excellent for me wherever I am."

It was true: Alik lived in Manhattan as he had lived in Moscow's Trubnaya Street or Ligovka, or in any of his long-stay or three-day addresses. He quickly made himself at home in new places, exploring their side-streets and dark spaces, their beautiful and perilous angles, like the body of a new lover.

In the years of his youth everything had whirled past him at great speed. But later, with his heightened attentiveness and memory, he found that nothing had been forgotten: he could recall the patterns of the wallpaper in every room he had lived in, the faces of the shopkeepers in all the local bakeries, the shape of the mouldings on the façade of the building opposite, the profile of a pike caught on a rod in Pleshcheevo lake in 1969, the lyre-shaped pine tree with one broken point rising over the pioneer camp in Verya where he used to spend his summers as a child. As if in gratitude for the memory, the world opened itself up to him. He went to Cape Cod, swollen from the rains, and a trembling sun poked through the clouds. He walked past an apple tree, and as though waiting for this moment, an apple dropped at his feet as a present. His life had a charmed quality which extended even to the world of technology: when he dialled a number on the telephone, the line was always free. It became a little trick of his: people who knew about it would sometimes ask him to dial a constantly engaged number. He would sometimes refuse for hours before suddenly seizing his moment and immediately getting through.

America returned his admiration with friendship. The newness of the New World took his breath away. It seemed new to him in the most literal sense of the word: even the oldest, many-ringed trees seemed to be made from newer, stronger material. Here everything was solid, firm, crude. Alik, a man of the third, Russian world, had by the age of thirty known both America and Europe. At first Vienna and Rome, the sweetness of Italy, under whose spell he had lived for almost a year. Only when he went to America and had lived there for several years did he understand the American envy of Old Europe, with its cultural subtlety, its worn, even worn-out, transparency, and also Europe's disdainful, but fundamentally envious, attitude to broad-shouldered, elemental America.

Alik, with his bristling ginger moustache and his hair tied at that time in a long, wiry ponytail, stood between these two worlds like a judge, and they couldn't have had a fairer one. He was not distinguished by impartiality; on the contrary he was unbelievably, passionately partial. He worshipped the highways of America, the patchwork crowds of New York's subway, which he considered the most beautiful in the world, the American street food and street music. Yet he also loved the small round fountains in the squares of Aix-en-Provence marking a delicate transition between France and Italy; he loved Romanesque architecture, and rejoiced whenever he came across remnants of it; he loved the filigree shores of the Greek islands, shaped like the leaves of maples and birches; he loved medieval Germany, which kept promising to reveal itself in Marburg or Nuremberg but never did, because everything that wasn't on the streets was to be found in the country's stunning museums, and German art totally eclipsed the Italian Renaissance. And German beer was excellent too.

He never felt the need to take one side, he stood on his own side, and in this place he loved both equally.

He muttered to Teeshirt a brief and it seemed to him insignificant remark about America and Europe, and he felt sad that he had become stupid and couldn't talk persuasively or coherently any more.

Maika listened thoughtfully, and said: "Do you like Russia, then?"

"Of course I do."

"So what do you like about it?" she persevered.

"Just because," he brushed her off.

Maika was cross; she hadn't learnt to make allowances for his illness. "God, you're just like the rest of them! Tell me properly, why? Everyone says things were terrible there."

Alik considered this: the question really was far from simple. "Shall I tell you a secret?"

She nodded.

"Bring your ear closer."

She leaned her ear to his mouth, almost closing it. "Nobody has the faintest idea why. The most intelligent people are just dissembling," he said.

"Dis-what?"

"Pretending."

"And you? Do you pretend?" Teeshirt said exultantly.

"I dissemble better than anyone else."

Irina glanced enviously at them; they both looked extremely pleased with themselves.

TWELVE

The landlord of the building was a louse. Alik was his first tenant and had been a thorn in his side for almost twenty years. He had moved in just as the place fell into the man's hands and the lofts became vacant. The run-down former factory district of Chelsea, vividly described in the writings of Alik's beloved O. Henry, had become increasingly fashionable. Next to it stood Greenwich Village, with its bohemian social life, its narcotic delights, its cheerful clubs and night-life, which spread out to the adjacent districts. In the past twenty years the price of accommodation had shot up at least tenfold, but Alik's rent was fixed and he still paid only four hundred a month, and was constantly late with it too.

The landlord lived in one of New York's wealthy suburbs and left everything to his superintendent, a paid job which combined the duties of both janitor and house-manager. The "super" here was called Claude, and he had worked in the building virtually since its occupation. Claude was a highly original man, half-French with a complicated history. From the stories he told Alik, Trinidad would surface, with an ocean yacht, and North Africa, with dangerous hunting-trips. Most of it he probably invented, yet one had the impression that his real life was no less interesting, and Alik would fill in the gaps, telling everyone he was a great card-sharp, that he had been arrested and imprisoned in a Turkish jail and had escaped in a hot-air balloon.

Twice, when things were particularly difficult, Claude, who wasn't without artistic and philanthropic interests, had bailed Alik out by buying his paintings. There aren't many superintendents who buy art. As well as this, Claude loved Nina. He would drop by to chat with her and she would make him coffee and occasionally lay out cards for a silly fortune-telling game, "find the queen." Not knowing a word of English when she arrived in this country, she had immediately started learning French. This peculiar idiocy was typical of her, and it was probably the reason Claude loved her so much. He too had his peculiarities, and unlike everyone else he preferred Nina to Alik.

Visiting usually in the first part of the day, Claude saw an element of strict order in her chaotic and disorderly life. She would get up at about one and utter a weak cry. Alik would make her coffee and take it into the bedroom with a glass of cold water. This was when he was working, so he rarely spoke to her then. She would come round slowly, take a long bath, anoint her face and body with various creams sent by a friend from Moscow—she didn't recognize the American ones—and pass a brush endlessly over her renowned hair; in her youth she had worked for several years as a model at one of Moscow's fashion houses, and she could never forget this marvellous time in her life.

Putting on a black kimono, she would shut herself in the bedroom again with some delightfully foolish activity: laying out patience maybe, or piecing together a huge jigsaw puzzle. It was usually then that Claude arrived. She would receive her guest in the kitchen and they would drink tiny cups of coffee, one after another. At this time of the day she was unable to eat or drink alcohol; she was terribly weak, and didn't even have the strength to start smoking until evening, when she had eaten something and poured her first vodka.

Alik would finish work at around seven. If they had money, they would eat in one of the little restaurants in Greenwich Village. Alik's first years in America were his most successful; there weren't so many Russian artists living in New York then, and he even enjoyed a small following.

From the start of her life in America Nina was crazy about everything oriental, and they would visit various Chinese or Japanese restaurants. Alik, of course, knew the most authentic ones. Before going out for the evening she would spend a long time dressing up and putting on her make-up. She would generally take her cat Katya with her on these outings. Pale-grey, with yellow eyes, Katya had been brought over from Moscow with all the proper papers, and was also mad: what normal cat would lie for hours across someone's shoulder, her paws languidly dangling down?

If guests came over they would order pizzas from the café downstairs, or Chinese food from their favourite restaurant in Chinatown, where the owner knew them and always sent over a small present for Nina. People would bring beer or vodka; there wasn't much hard drinking then. "It's the climate," Alik used to say. "There's no hard drinking in this country, only alcoholism."

It was true: by Nina's third year in America she was an

alcoholic, even though she didn't drink much, and her beauty became even more startling.

The landlord had arrived in the city the previous day to put his affairs in order. He docked Claude's pay for a garbage fine, and demanded Alik's immediate eviction on the grounds of his three months' arrears. Claude tried to defend his oldest resident, citing his terrible illness and apparently imminent death.

"I'll see for myself," the landlord declared, and Claude had no option but to take him up to the fifth floor.

It was eleven o'clock and things were in full swing as they got out of the lift. Nobody paid any attention to the bulky old man with the pink, chamois-leather face. There was none of the rowdy merriment and specifically Russian drunkenness he had expected; instead, a large crowd of people were huddled in front of the television. He looked around. He hadn't been up here for a while. It was a good apartment; fix it up and it would fetch at least thirty-five hundred, maybe forty.

"He's a fine artist, this guy," Claude glanced at the canvases stacked against the wall; Alik never liked hanging up his paintings, his old work got in his way.

The landlord peered briefly at them; a friend of his in Chelsea had run a cheap boarding-house here in the twenties. It was more of a flop-house really, and he had let all sorts of riff-raff in, impoverished artists, out-of-work actors. Somehow the place had survived the depression. A few times, out of the goodness of his heart, the man had let his artists give him paintings instead of rent, and he had hung them up in the hall. Years passed, and he turned out to own a collection worth a dozen boarding-houses. But that was a long time ago; times had changed, artists were two a penny now. "No, no, I don't want any of these paintings," he decided.

Nina saw Claude at the entrance and wandered over to him with her elegant, unsteady gait, preparing some French phrase for him. But she didn't have the chance to use it, because Claude said, "Our landlord's here on business."

Nina displayed an unexpected command of the situation. Muttering something to him she darted to Libin, grasped his head in her hands and whispered urgently in his ear: "Our landlord's here, the super brought him. You must make sure they don't get near Alik. Please, I'm begging you."

Libin quickly took in what was happening and went over to the landlord grinning imbecilically. "We're all a little bit concerned, there's a political coup going on in Moscow, you see." He spoke as though he were prime minister of some neighbouring state. As he did so he pushed them towards the lift with his belly. They didn't resist. By the lift he finally stopped smiling and said very distinctly: "I'm Alik's brother. I apologise for the arrears, I paid all the rent yesterday and I guarantee it won't happen again."

Now the damned Irishman will start ranting, Claude thought. But without saying a word the landlord pressed the button of the lift.

THIRTEEN

For two days and nights they didn't switch off the television. For two days and nights the telephone didn't stop ringing. The door banged incessantly. Alik lay flat and rubbery, like an empty hot-water bottle, but his mind was alert and he assured everyone he was feeling better.

Like a classical drama, the plot had unfolded for three days. In that time the past, from which they had more or less totally cut themselves off, came back into their lives and they were horrified. They wept, searched for familiar faces in the crowds outside the White House, and were rewarded by the moment when Lyuda's son suddenly yelled: "Look, there's Dad!"

On the screen a bearded man in glasses, who looked somehow familiar to everyone, was walking towards the camera with his head bowed.

Lyuda clutched her throat with both hands: "It's Kostya! I knew he'd be there!"

By this time it was obvious that the coup hadn't succeeded.

"We've won," Alik said.

It was unclear who "we" was, but it was the same "we" Father Victor had discovered to his surprise in Paris at the start of the Second World War. His grandfather, a White officer who had become a priest after emigrating, began to feel this sharp connection with Russia then. All of a sudden, the "they," for whom his feelings had been hardening during his years in exile, had become that same "we," very nearly causing him to return home in 1947 to certain death.

Libin disagreed with Alik but he wasn't going to argue, and merely murmured, "Well it's not clear who's won, in fact."

Everyone was just happy that civil war had been averted, and that the tanks had left the city.

The news bulletins continued uninterruptedly: on Lyubyanka Square they toppled the statue to Dzerzhinsky and showed the empty plinth. The finest monument to Soviet power was an empty pedestal; the party, which had immortalized itself in granite, marble and steel, had crumbled to dust and vanished like an hallucination.

Three people were killed and buried, three grains of sand picked from the crowd by a heavenly hand, three young men with good faces, a Russian, a Ukrainian, a Jew. Over two of them they waved incense, the third was covered with a prayer shawl. There were thousands and thousands of people. There had never been such funerals in this country. It was as though everything sick, rotten and wicked was being thrown away like slops, a bucket of stinking rubbish floating down the river.

The people sitting here now, former Russians, were unanimously happy, and they celebrated not by drinking more than usual but by singing old Soviet songs. Best of all sang Valentina:

Around us all is blue and green
Under the window the nightingales sing . . .

There was nothing blue and green in this neighbourhood, this apartment, their lives here had other nuances, other degrees of intensity, yet each recalled the colours of their childhood: Valentina remembered Institute Street in Kaluga, running between two rows of pale lime trees to the soapy-blue Oka; Alik remembered the blues and greens of Moscow Province, the diffident, sweetly trusting colours of the spring foliage and the long tender shadows across the sky; Faika remembered her village, its lank back gardens, and the clumsy golden church domes against the bright-green hedge.

Outside the window the Paraguayan music dragged on, not the salsa now but something wild and mindless, banging and howling. Alik was more sensitive to music than the others. "For Christ's sake go and shut them up," he begged Libin.

Libin grabbed Natasha and left.

On the television more crowds appeared. In the room there were also crowds of people, and it seemed to Alik that the two were connected. At times among the familiar faces an unfamiliar one would flash past. He glimpsed a small grey old man in strange white clothes, with a leather strap around his forehead, not quite in focus.

"Nina, who's that old fellow?" he asked.

Nina started, wondering if he had noticed the landlord.

"See, that little one with the white beard."

Nina looked, but the old man had disappeared.

The unbearable music disappeared too, and in its place came children, a large number of strange, unfriendly children with animal faces. Despite the lateness of the evening, it was very hot.

Valentina came to Alik. "What would you like?"

"Sing me something cool."

She sat next to him, embraced his inert leg and sang quietly and very clearly:

> *Frost, frost, do not freeze me*
> *Do not freeze my horse or me . . .*

Her voice was cool, and ripples from it spread through the air like a toy boat being lowered into the water. Alik saw himself bundled in his old thick brown fur coat tied by the belt with his favourite buckle. His head was covered by a tight beaver-lamb cap on top of a white kerchief, and he was sitting in his old sledge with the bent back. Walking in front of him he saw his mother's felt boots, and the hem of her blue coat flapping against the grey of the felt. A woollen scarf was tied tightly over his mouth. The scarf was wet and warm, and he had to breathe hard, very hard, because the moment he stopped an icy crust would seal the moist, warm gap and the scarf would freeze and hurt him.

There were more children now, and they were wearing fur coats too, fluffy and covered in snow.

The door banged, and Libin tumbled out of the lift with the six Paraguayans. They were short, dressed in black trousers and white shirts, and banging castanets, rattles and drums.

"Nina, who are these people?" Alik asked uncertainly.

"Libin's brought them."

Libin was very drunk. He came up to Alik. "Hey, look at these wonderful guys! I took them for a drink. I thought they wouldn't be able to play if they had a glass in their hands, and I was right! They're wonderful guys, but they don't know any English. One of them can say a few words, the others don't even speak much Spanish, their language is Guarani or something. We had a drink and I told them my friend was ill, and they said they had some special music for people who are ill. How about it? They're wonderful guys."

The Paraguayans had already formed themselves into a line. Their leader, who had a scar across his brick-red face, struck his drum and they moved around in a circle, swaying rhythmically and emitting a strange half-gulp, half-yell, bending their short legs at every step.

The women, who in recent weeks had been so exasperated by their noise, now collapsed into silent laughter. Yet here in the apartment it sounded quite different, eerily serious, reminiscent not of street music but of other, immeasurably greater things. In it was the beat of the heart, the breath of the lungs, the movement of water, the growl of the digestion. Heavens, even their instruments were skulls and bones, and skeletons hung from them like festive decorations. The music finally died away, but before people had time to murmur together in the pause, the men turned to face the other way, still in single file and made another circle, and another kind of music started up, ancient and macabre.

The dance of death, Alik thought.

Suddenly its meaning was revealed to him as the story of the dying body, and the musicians' movements as part of the prologue to some theme which would follow. The monotonous and doleful sounds which had so irritated him for weeks past now appeared as familiar as the alphabet, but they broke off, leaving something unsaid.

More and more guests arrived. He saw in the crowd his old school physics teacher, Nikolai Vasilevich, known as the Galosh, and he felt a weary surprise that the man had emigrated at his age. How old would he be now? He saw his classmate Kolka Zaitsev, who had been killed falling under a tram, a thin boy in a ski-jacket with pockets, kicking a soft rag ball in front of him; how sweet that he had brought it along. He saw his cousin Musya, who had died of leukaemia as a child, walking across the room with a washing-up bowl in her hands, only she wasn't a child now but almost grown up. None of this seemed at all strange to him, but in the correct order of things; there was even a sense of old injustices being put right.

Fima came and touched his cold hand. "Maybe you should come back now, Alik?"

"Okay," Alik agreed.

Fima gathered up his light body and carried him to the bedroom. His lips were blue, and his fingernails were a paler blue, but his hair burned with its unchanging dark copper colour.

"Hypoxia," Fima noted automatically.

Nina took one of the bottles from the window-sill. The chief Paraguayan, who was their interpreter, went over to Valentina and asked her if he could touch her hair. With one hand he felt his own rough locks, gleaming like coal, and with the other he ran his fingers through her tinted, many-coloured tresses, and he laughed with delight; two weeks ago they had left their village in the rainforest and had come to New York, and he hadn't yet managed to touch all the wonders of this new world. Valentina had the strange sensation that someone was putting a skullcap on her head, but there was nothing unpleasant about it and it soon passed.

Alik was fighting for air. He knew that he must breathe as deeply as possible, otherwise the warm gap in his scarf would close. He breathed in convulsively, rather more often than he breathed out.

"I'm tired," he said.

Fima held his wrist, dry as the branch of a dead tree. The diaphragm muscle was dying now, the lungs were dying, the heart. Fima opened his medical bag and pondered. He could give Alik a camphor injection, drive on his exhausted heart and make it gallop for a while. Or morphine maybe, a blissful oblivion from which he wouldn't return. Or things could just take their course. In that case he wouldn't live more than a day, two at most. There was no knowing how many hours he might last.

This country hated suffering; it rejected it ontologically, admitting it only as an incident which must be instantly eradicated. This young, suffering denying nation had developed whole schools—philosophical, psychological and medical—dedicated to the single problem of how to save people from suffering. Fima's Russian brain had difficulty in coping with this concept. The land which had raised him loved and valued suffering, and derived its nourishment from it: from suffering people grew, developed, became wise. Fima's Jewish blood, filtered for millennia through suffering, carried within it an extra vital substance which disintegrated in its absence; people like him lost touch with the earth under their feet when released from suffering.

But none of this applied now to Alik; Fima didn't want his friend to suffer so cruelly during the last hours of his life.

"We'd better call the ambulance, Nina," he said, more resolutely than he felt.

FOURTEEN

The ambulance arrived fifteen minutes later, and a skinny intellectual in glasses appeared with a robust young black man built like a basketball player, with a jutting jaw. He was the doctor; the other man was probably a runaway Pole or Czech, Fima decided, who also hadn't managed to pass his American exams. He found the similarities unwelcome and unpleasant, and he walked to the window.

The doctor threw the sheet off Alik and passed his hands in front of his eyes. Alik didn't respond. The doctor took his wrist, which drowned in his large hand like a pencil, and the sentence he uttered was long and incomprehensible. Fima guessed that he was talking about respirators and hospitalization, but he couldn't make out if he was suggesting they take Alik or was refusing to take him.

Nina tossed her hair and declared in Russian that she

wasn't letting Alik go anywhere. The doctor peered at her exhausted beauty, then, lowering his remarkable lashes over his eyes, said, "I understand, Ma'am."

Drawing three ampoules of liquid into a large syringe, he injected Alik between the skin and bone of his almost nonexistent thigh.

The man in glasses stopped writing, knitted his shaggy, long-suffering brows on his beaky face and said to the doctor in an accent which seemed even to Fima to be atrocious: "The lady's in a bad way, we'd better give her a sedative or something, seeing as . . ."

The doctor pulled off his gloves, threw them in his case without looking at his assistant, and muttered a contemptuous remark. It tore Fima apart; he would have liked to do something to him. "Why am I sitting here like a prick? I'm not staying, I'm going back," he thought for the first time in all these wretched years, and suddenly he felt afraid. Could he ever go back to being a real doctor? Would he be able to pass all those damned exams in Russian? Who would need them in Kharkov anyway, with his diploma?

As soon as the useless medical team had left, Nina became very agitated. Dashing to her bottles again, she sat at the bottom of Alik's bed and poured oil into her palms, rubbing his feet, from the tips of his toes up his legs to his thighs.

She poured handful after handful from the bottle. "They understand nothing, Alik, nothing. No one understands anything, they don't believe in anything. But I believe. Lord, I believe." Splashes of oil flew around, spreading on the sheet as she rubbed his legs, his chest. "Alik, Alik, do something, say something. Damn the night, you'll be better tomorrow, you'll see."

Alik said nothing, just took a few laboured, shuddering breaths.

"You lie down for a bit, Nina, and I'll massage him, okay?" Fima said, and she agreed surprisingly easily. "Gioia's keeping watch in the studio. She wanted to be on duty tonight. Maybe you could sleep on the carpet for a while and she could sit here?"

"Gioia can clear off, he doesn't need anyone." Nina lay down with her face by Alik's feet, stretching across the wide bed in which he was already completely lost, and speaking to him: "We'll go to Jamaica, we'll visit Florida, we'll hire a big car and take everyone with us, Valentina, Libin, everyone. We'll visit Disneyland too, right, Alik? We'll have a wonderful time. We'll stay in motels, just like we used to. They don't understand a thing, these doctors. We'll cure you with herbs, the herbs will get you on your feet, they've raised worse than you!"

"Try to sleep a little now, Nina," Fima urged.

She nodded: "Bring me a drink."

Fima went to fix her drink. The guests had departed.

In a corner of the studio Gioia nursed her little grey Dostoyevsky, waiting to be called. One of the remaining guests slept on, his head covered in a blanket. Lyuda finished washing the glasses and looked at Fima. "It's the final agony," he told her.

He brought Nina her drink. She drank it, curled up at Alik's feet again, muttered something inaudible, and fell asleep. It seemed she still didn't understand what was happening.

Tomorrow, or rather today, was a working day for Fima. The day after he could take off, the day after that he probably wouldn't be needed any more. He sat on the bed and spread wide his bumpy knees with their shaggy carpet of hair, a clumsy, tedious man, a failure. There was nothing he could do now but sit here sadly sipping vodka and orange, wetting Alik's lips—Alik was unable to swallow now—and wait for the inevitable.

Close to morning Alik's fingers started shaking slightly, and Fima decided the time had come to wake Nina. He stroked her head and she returned slowly from somewhere far away: as always it took her a long time to understand where she had been brought back to. "Nina, wake up!" he said as her eyes finally came to life.

She leaned over her husband and was astonished yet again by the changes that had taken place in him during the short time she had been asleep. His face was now that of a fourteen-year-old boy, childish, bright and calm. But his breathing was almost inaudible.

"Alik." She stroked his head, his neck. "Oh, Alik."

There had always been something supernatural about his responsiveness. He would answer her call instantly and from any distance. He would telephone her from another town at the very moment when she was longing for him and needed him most. Now, for the first time, her voice failed to reach him.

"What's wrong, Fima? What's happening?"

Fima clasped her thin shoulders. "He's dying, Nina."

And she knew it was true.

Her transparent eyes lit up. Pulling herself together, she said to Fima with unexpected firmness: "Go out and don't come back in here for a while."

Fima went out without saying a word.

FIFTEEN

Lyuda stood irresolutely at the door, looking in.

"Go away all of you, all of you!" Nina's gesture was majestic, even theatrical.

Gioia sat in the corner resting her chin on her knee, and said in surprise: "But Nina, I was going to sit with him."

"Everybody out, I said!"

Gioia flushed, shook herself and ran to the lift. Lyuda stood distractedly in the middle of the studio. The sleeping guest snored on with the blanket over his head.

Nina ran to the kitchen and groped in the back of the cupboard for a white porcelain soup tureen.

For a moment she recalled the marvellous day in Washington when they had bought it. They had been staying with their friend Slavka Crane, a cheerful double-bass player who had retrained as a sad computer programmer. They had eaten breakfast in a small restaurant near a little square in the Alexandria district. Some pensioners were playing astoundingly bad

112

but free music on the street, and afterwards Slavka had taken them off to an open-air market. It was such a happy day that they decided to buy something beautiful, but for a few cents (as always, they were very short of money), and a handsome grey-haired black man with a withered arm had sold them this English soup tureen dating from the time of the Boston tea party. They had spent the rest of the day dragging around with them this large, inconvenient object which they couldn't fit in their bag, and Slavka had gone in his car to meet someone or see them off.

"This is why we bought it," Nina thought now, filling it with water.

Drawing herself up to her full height, she solemnly carried it into the bedroom, holding it to her face and pressing her lips against its sides.

She's really crazy now, Fima frowned, what will she do next? She had already forgotten that she had just sent everyone out.

She placed the bowl carefully on the stool, took three candles out of the cupboard, lit them and melted their bases, then stuck them to the porcelain rim of the bowl. She did all this quickly and effortlessly; it was as though everything she needed was coming out to meet her.

She took the paper icon from the wall and smiled, remembering the strange man who had left it there. He was one of the many homeless emigrés who had stayed with them. Although Nina had been generally indifferent to their guests and barely noticed them, this one she had asked Alik to send away. But Alik had merely said, "Shut up, Nina, we live too well." He was an odd, mad young man. He didn't wash and wore what appeared to be chains on his body. He hated America, and the only reason he had come was that he had had a vision that Christ was living there, and he had come to find Him. He chased around Central Park all day looking for Him, then someone helped him to see the light, and he went to California, to a fellow seeker, an American this time—Serafim or Sebastian or something—also mad, apparently, and a monk.

Nina propped the icon against the bowl, gazed at Alik and thought for a moment. Something troubled her—his name. His name was a problem: although people always called him Alik, he had been registered as Abraham in honour of his dead grandfather. Before his parents divorced, they had quarrelled about whose idea it had been to give their child this stupid, provocative name; even some of his closest friends didn't know his real name, particularly since he had put it down as Alik on his American papers.

Whatever the name, the man destined to bear it hadn't much longer to live. He gasped convulsively from time to time. Nina rushed to the bookshelf, looking for a church calendar. At random, she pulled out the right volume from behind a jumble of books. For 22 August she read: "Martyrs Fotii and Anikita, Pamphil and Kapiton. Holy Martyr Alexander." Everything was right again, the name was right; everything was coming out to meet her again. She smiled.

"Alik!" she cried. "Please don't be angry or offended, I'm going to baptize you."

She took from her long neck the gold cross that used to belong to her grandmother, a Ters cossack. Maria Ignatevna had told her what to do. Any Christian could do it if someone was dying; just a cross made with water or sand, a gold cross, or even some matches tied in a cross. Now she just had to say a few simple words she had memorized. She crossed herself, dipped the cross in the water and said in a hoarse voice: "In the name of the Father, the Son and the Holy Ghost . . ." She made the sign of the cross in the water, dipped her hand in, scooped up a handful of water and sprinkled it over her husband's face. ". . . I baptize thee, Alik, servant of God."

At the critical moment she didn't notice that the truly suitable name of Alexander had flown out of her head.

She was unsure what to do next. With the cross in one hand she sat beside him rubbing the baptismal water over his face and chest. One of the candles bent over the rim of the bowl and, in defiance of the laws of physics, fell inside the now holy vessel. It spluttered and went out. Nina laid the cross on his neck. "Alik, Alik!" she called.

He didn't respond, just gave a throaty snore and fell silent.

"Fima!" she shouted.

Fima walked in.

"Look what I've done. I've baptized him."

Fima retained his professionalism. "Well, fine. He certainly can't get any worse."

The marvellous feeling of certainty she had had earlier suddenly deserted her. Moving the stool back to the corner, she lay down beside Alik and gabbled something Fima couldn't understand.

The door opened slightly and Kipling the dog walked in. For the past three days he had lain by the door waiting for his master to return. He laid his head on the bed. I should take him out, Fima thought; it's time for me to go to work. Gioia had gone off offended. Lyuda too had left in the night. Fima roused the sleeping man in the corner, who turned out to be Shmuel, not Libin, as Fima had supposed, which was just as well, since Shmuel was in no hurry to go anywhere; he had spent his entire ten years in America on welfare. Fima hastily explained to him the emergency procedures and left his telephone number at work. Now he would take Kipling out, who was waiting patiently by the door wagging his tail. After that he must go to work.

SIXTEEN

⌒The day after baptizing Alik, Nina didn't leave the bed-room. She lay there clasping his legs, not letting people in. "Quiet, quiet, he's sleeping," she said when anyone came to the door.

He was in an oblivious state, drawing the occasional wheezing breath. He could hear everything that was going on around him but as though from a great distance, and he wanted to tell people that everything was all right; but the scarf was tied more tightly now, and he couldn't dislodge it.

At the same time he was assailed by new sensations. He felt light and insubstantial like a cloud, as though he were moving in a black-and-white film, only the black wasn't black and the white wasn't white, rather everything consisted of shades of grey because the film was old and grainy. There was nothing unpleasant about it. This movement, which he had longed for all these months, felt blissful, almost drug-induced. Familiar shadows were glimpsed on the edges of a washed-out

117

road. Some resembled wooden silhouettes, others had human form. Once again he saw his old teacher Nikolai Vasilevich, the Galosh, and he noted with satisfaction that the appearance of this man, a mathematician of sober and severe intellect, proved that what was happening was real and released him from a vague unease that this might be a dream, or an hallucination. Nikolai Vasilevich clearly recognized him and made a welcoming gesture, and Alik saw that he was coming towards him.

Nina was jingling her bottles again, but there was something pleasant and musical about the sound. Pouring the dregs of some bitter infusion into her hands she whispered something inaudible, but it didn't bother him. The Galosh was beside him now, silently smacking his lips as he used to at school; Alik had forgotten this habit of his, and he remembered it now with a feeling of tenderness. It was all terribly convincing: no, it wasn't a dream, it was really happening.

In the middle of the day a plumber arrived to install the new air-conditioner. An incurious mulatto festooned with gold chains, he was accompanied by an unhealthy-looking young assistant (one of Alik's friends was paying). Nina let them into the bedroom. They worked quickly without so much as glancing at the dying man, and the heat in the room was replaced by a dusty cool. Soon Valentina arrived. Nina wouldn't let her into the bedroom, so she sat in the studio beside the tear-stained Gioia.

In a corner Maika lay on the grimy white carpet with a blanket folded under her head, reading *The Tibetan Book of Living and Dying* in English. She dreamed of reading it in the original. Since yesterday she had regretted that she hadn't been born a man and couldn't go to a Tibetan monastery, and had even asked her mother that morning if she could have an operation to make her bust smaller, thus bringing her closer to the beautiful life of a Buddhist monk.

Nina pushed some pillows beneath Alik's back, raising him in the bed so that he was almost sitting up. She moistened his parched, dark lips and tried to blow a little water through them with a straw, but it leaked out of the corners.

"Alik, Alik!" she called him, touched him, stroked him. She put her lips to his iliac crest and drew her tongue across to his navel, along the line which divides the human body in two. The smell of him was strange, his skin tasted bitter; she had been marinating him in this bitterness for two months now.

She buried her face in the red tendrils of his pubic hair; his hair didn't change, she thought.

She finally stopped bothering him, and Alik suddenly said very clearly: "Nina, I'm completely better now."

At eight o'clock in the evening when Fima returned from work, he saw a strange sight: Nina was sitting naked on her black kimono facing Alik, wiping her fine arms with the thick residue from one of the bottles and saying: "See how it's helping, it's such a good herb."

Dreamily she raised her shining eyes to Fima and said solemnly, "Alik told me he's better now."

"He's dead," Fima thought. He touched Alik's hand; it was empty, the drumbeats had gone out of it.

Going out of the bedroom, he poured himself half a glass of cheap vodka from a large bottle with a handle, gulped it down, then walked to the other end of the studio and back again. At this time of day there weren't many people around, they tended to come later. No one looked at Fima. Valentina and Libin were playing with Alik's backgammon. Gioia was laying out the Tarot as Nina had taught her, trying to bring some clarity into her already clear and solitary life. Faika was eating fried eggs with mayonnaise on them; she ate everything with mayonnaise. Moscow Lyuda had long since washed all the dishes and was sitting with her son by the television waiting for news from home.

"Alyosha, switch that thing off, Alik's dead," Fima said quietly to the young man, so quietly that nobody heard him. "Hey everyone, Alik's dead," he repeated, still very quietly.

The lift clanged, and Irina came in.

"Alik's dead," he told her, and at last everyone heard.

"Already?" Valentina burst out in anguish, as though Alik had promised her that he would live for ever, and had broken this promise with his untimely death.

"Oh shit!" Maika said, throwing aside her book and running to the lift, almost knocking her mother off her feet as she went.

Irina stood by the door, rubbing her hurt shoulder. Maybe I'll visit Russia for a week, she thought, I'll look up the Kazantsevs, Gisya (Gisya was Alik's older sister). She must be an old woman now, she's fourteen years older than him. She always loved me.

Gioia dropped her cards and wept.

For some reason everyone started putting on clothes. Valentina dived head-first into a long Indian skirt. Lyuda found her sandals. They all made for the bedroom. Fima stopped them. "Wait, Nina doesn't know yet, we must tell her."

"You tell her," Libin begged. He and Fima hadn't been talking to each other for three years, and now he didn't even notice himself asking.

120

Fima opened the bedroom door; everything was exactly the same. Alik lay with the orange sheet pulled up to his chin, Nina sat on the floor rubbing her narrow feet with their long toes, repeating over and over again: "They're good herbs, Alik, they have immense power."

Kipling was there too, resting his forepaws and his sad, wise face on the bed.

How stupid it is to think that dogs are afraid of dead people, Fima thought.

He pulled Nina up, picked her soaked kimono off the floor and threw it over her shoulders. She didn't resist.

"He's dead," Fima said again, and felt as though he had already lived for a long time in this new world in which Alik was no longer around.

Nina looked at him with watchful, transparent eyes, and smiled; her face was tired but cunning. "Alik's better, you know."

He led her out of the bedroom. Valentina was already bringing her her drink. She drank and smiled a worldly smile at no one in particular: "Do you know, Alik's better! He told me himself!"

Gioia made a sound like a laugh and ran into the kitchen with her hand over her mouth. From below, somebody buzzed the intercom. Nina sat in the armchair with a bright, distracted face, pushing the ice around her glass with a cocktail-stick.

This was how Ophelia must have looked. Her defence, like a good boxer's, was to refuse to know anything. Everything was all right. Alik couldn't leave her; she had always lived outside reality and he had covered for her madness.

There was method in this madness, Irina thought. She had nothing more to do here; she must leave now, without delay.

121

She went down in the lift. Maika wasn't waiting by the door; her daughter had gone.

Dodging through the slow stream of traffic, she went into the café opposite.

"Whiskey?" the shrewd black barman asked, pouring her a glass.

Of course, he's Alik's friend, she thought. Pointing to the house opposite she said: "He's dead."

The man knew at once who she was talking about. He raised his sculpted hands with their silver rings and bracelets, and wrinkled his Jamaican face. "Oh Lord, why do you take the best from us?" he said.

He splashed himself something from a thick bottle, drank quickly and said to Irina, "Listen girl, how's Nina? I want to give her some money."

No one had called Irina "girl" for a very long time. And suddenly she realized it was as if Alik had never emigrated. He had built his Russia around him, a Russia which hadn't existed for a long time and perhaps never had. He was carefree and ir-responsible, people didn't live like that here, they didn't live like it anywhere, dammit. How to define this charm, which had captivated even her little girl? He hadn't done anything special for anyone, yet they would all have gone through fire for him. No, she didn't understand, she didn't understand.

She went to the phone-booth at the back of the café, in-serted her card and keyed in a long number. At Harris' home, the machine picked up her call. At his office his old secretary, who reminded Irina of a monkey, told her he was busy. "Put me through," Irina said, giving her name.

Harris was instantly on the line.

"I'm free this weekend," she said.

"Ring me from the airport and I'll meet you." His voice was cool, but Irina could tell he was happy.

His dry, ruddy face and neat moustache, his mirror-like bald patch, a sofa, a glass and a slice of lemon, eleven minutes of love—you could count them on your watch—and a feeling of total security as she rested her head on his broad, hairy chest. It was all very serious, and must be taken to its logical conclusion . . .

SEVENTEEN

The past couldn't be cancelled. Well, why would anyone want to cancel it, anyway.

Irina had done her last performance in Boston, and without going back to the hotel she had gone straight to the airport. There she bought herself a ticket, and two hours later she was in New York. The year was 1975. After paying for her ticket she had forty dollars left, which she had brought from Russia in the pocket of her trousers. It was a good thing she had, because the troupe had not been given any cash; they had been promised some money on their last day for shopping, but Irina couldn't wait any longer.

As she sat in the plane, she looked at her watch and imagined the scandal that would break next morning. This evening the sweaty managers would rush through the sleazy boarding-house banging on doors and asking people when they had last seen her. There would be curses and anathemas, the head of personnel would get fired for sure. Her retired father would try to wriggle out of it and do deals, but her wise mother would be pleased. I'll ring her tomorrow, Irina thought; I'll tell her everything's worked out brilliantly, there's no need for her to worry.

In New York she called Pereira, the circus manager, who had promised to help her. He wasn't in; it turned out that he had left town and forgotten to tell her. The other number she had on her belonged to Ray, a clown she had met three years earlier at a circus festival in Prague. He was at home. She explained to him with some difficulty who she was. Her name clearly meant nothing to him, but he invited her over.

Her first night in New York passed in a dream. Ray lived in a tiny apartment in the Village with his friend, a graceful young man who opened the door to her in a lady's swimsuit. They proved to be extraordinarily good young men and did everything they could to help her. Later, Ray admitted that he had had no memory of her, and wasn't even sure if he had been in Prague.

Butane—Irina wasn't sure if this was the flatmate's surname, his first name or a nickname—had already lived illegally in America for five years, so her insane step didn't seem so insane to them. They had no work or money at the time, and no idea how they were going to pay the rent. Next morning they paid it with Irina's money, then they all set off to perform for the summer visitors in Central Park. Here too, according to them, Irina brought them luck. For the next few days she contorted her body on a mat, then she sewed five cloth puppets, which she put on her hands, feet and head, and their earnings became entirely satisfactory. Irina slept modestly on three sofa cushions in the room next to Ray's, trying not to inhibit his sexual freedom. But before long Butane started getting close to her and Ray grew jealous. For a while their triple alliance hung in the balance. Irina still went out to work with them, but she realized she must find another way of living here. They were great boys though, and completely reconciled her to casting off her old skin: it turned out that half of America was made up of people like her.

Then one August day, having finished her solo act by the entrance to the small zoo at Central Park, she suddenly found herself in the arms of Alik, who for the last twenty minutes had been watching the happy play of her double-jointed limbs.

Half an hour later she was sitting with him in his loft, which hadn't been partitioned into separate rooms then. He had lived for two years in America and was working hard and selling respectably. He was happy and independent, emigration suited him. He looked at this small, fast-moving animal with the impetuous human face, and he realized what had been missing from his life.

Seven years had passed since they parted in Moscow, seven wasted years, and they had to make up for them as quickly as possible in gestures, words and feelings. Twenty-four hours a day weren't enough for them; everything was as transparent as glass, they didn't feel the ground under their feet.

One night as they were returning home they had found a large white carpet left outside some rich person's house. They dragged it up to the apartment and Irina would sit on it in her habitual lotus position holding her English textbook in front of her, studying her grammar, while Alik worked away on his pomegranates. His loft was full of them: pink, crimson and brown, squishy and rotten, or the shrivelled corpses sucked dry of the burning juice.

In Alik's pictures of this time the pomegranates appeared singly, in pairs or in groups, with different elongations and foreshortenings. It almost seemed as though in producing these simple changes he might reveal new, undiscovered numbers within the known numerical sequence—between seven and eight, say.

Irina lived for eighty-eight days in Alik's studio. They ate, talked, made love, took warm showers—that summer too had been hot, and the pipes had heated—and everything was happiness, or rather the beginning of happiness, because it was impossible to imagine that it would ever end. Scott Joplin's compositions spilled through the night air.

Irina's lips swelled with softness: she knew immediately that she was pregnant, her whole body from her head to her feet was filled with a new physical happiness. Alik didn't know; if he had, he might have acted differently. As it was, he was awaiting the arrival of Nina. He had divorced her before he left Russia, although he wasn't sure if this had been a joke or for real. Since her father would never give her permission to leave while he was alive, Alik had decided to go alone. His departure tipped Nina over the edge of her quiet madness, and she had tried to kill herself (it was her second suicide attempt). She sat in the hospital making endless telephone calls and finally found a phoney American who was prepared to marry her, after which she applied to live with him permanently in America; such documents often involved years of running around.

Irina and Alik were sitting in the loft one evening. Alik took a knife and sliced a large red watermelon in two. It fell apart and the telephone rang. It was Nina, announcing that she had received permission to leave and had bought her ticket.

"Well, I don't really see how I can get out of it now," Alik said, putting down the phone.

For Irina the whole thing came as a total surprise.

"She can't survive without me, she's so weak," Alik explained.

Irina was strong. Hadn't she walked on her hands to the edge of the roof? She wasn't afraid of bosses or the authorities. He proposed renting a room for her with some friends of his on Staten Island, while he thought of a way to extricate himself from the whole crazy mess. He hadn't reckoned on Irina's pride, which had grown no less in the years they had been apart. A week before Nina arrived, when everything had been arranged with his friends, she left Alik's apartment, as she thought for ever.

EIGHTEEN

Irina came out of the café and stood on the street, wondering what to do next; she must go home, Teeshirt was probably there already.

Just then a van with an air-conditioner on the roof drove up to the doorway of Alik's building and parked under the "No Standing At Any Time" sign. Two young men in uniforms jumped out, followed by a third man resembling a bald Charlie Chaplin, who minced after them with a suitcase.

"The corpse-carrier," Irina thought. "I'm going home."

Fima met the undertakers. Some stage management was required. He nodded to Valentina: "Keep Nina in the studio."

But Nina wasn't going anywhere; she sat in the battered

armchair and muttered enigmatically, mentioning herbs, Alik's character and God's will.

The two sturdy young men and their puny boss shut themselves in the bedroom with Fima; it was sad that Alik couldn't laugh at this comical trio, he thought.

As they were running through the funeral arrangements, the two young men pulled from the suitcase a large black plastic bag, like the rubbish bags that line the streets every evening, and with three deft movements they slipped Alik inside as though putting shopping in a carrier bag. Charlie Chaplin stood watching.

"Stop, wait a minute," Fima said. "I don't want his wife to see."

He went to the studio, pulled the unresisting Nina from her chair and carried her into the kitchen. Holding her gently against him, he brushed his unshaven cheek against her long neck, etched with tiny wrinkles, and said: "Well Bunny rabbit, what can I get you? Shall I run out for some grass?"

"No, I don't want to smoke, I want another drink."

He clasped her wrist and held it for a moment.

"Do you want me to give you an injection? A nice little injection?" He stood barring the kitchen door with his broad back, trying to decide on the best cocktail to knock her out and disconnect her for a bit. As he did so the undertakers carried out the black bag, as though taking out the rubbish.

Irina was already heading for the subway as the workers opened the boot of the van and pushed the black bag inside.

Fima gave Nina an injection, and soon her eyes closed and she slept until morning on the same orange sheet from which they had just removed her husband. It was strange, but she didn't once ask where he was, she merely smiled tenderly from time to time before falling asleep, and said, "You never listen to me, I told you he would get better."

People kept coming. Some didn't know he had died, and had just come over to visit. A number of his friends arrived, including several from outside the city's Russian-Jewish community. There was an Italian singer, one of Alik's friends from Rome, and the owner of the café opposite, who brought Nina a cheque as he had promised. Libin, in accordance with Russian tradition, collected money. Some people from Moscow came, one with a letter for Alik, another saying he was an old friend. Some street people whom nobody knew turned up. The telephone rang, with calls from Paris and Yaroslavl.

Father Victor, when he learned of Alik's deathbed baptism, gesticulated in the air, shook his head and then said that everything was God's will. What else could an honourable Orthodox man say?

That morning, the day before the funeral, he picked Nina up in his old motorcar and drove her to the empty church— there were no services that day—and performed a funeral service for the dead man in his absence, who had been baptized virtually in his absence too.

In a low, resonant voice the priest chanted the best of all words, invented for just this eventuality. Nina shone with angelic beauty. Valentina stood holding a candle behind her in a dusty shaft of light from the ceiling window, and absolved herself for having loved this other woman's husband.

As the last echoes of Father Victor's voice died away in the dust-filled air, Valentina took from his hands a square packet containing some earth, a white ribbon with a prayer, and a small reproduction of an icon to put in the coffin. Then she grasped Nina's trembling arm and pushed her into a taxi.

Nina inclined her small head as she got into the battered yellow jalopy, as though it were a Rolls-Royce taking her to a reception at Buckingham Palace. This little bird has landed on my head, Valentina sighed. Lord, did I really hate her for so many years?

NINETEEN

The owners of Robins the Undertakers—formerly the Rabinoviches—had broken with traditional Jewish inflexibility in favour of a more humane and commercially justified tolerance. In the last fifty years the Jewish Funeral Society had become simply a funeral parlour, with four separate halls in which the sometimes exotic ceremonies of the different religions could take place. Only last week Mr Robins had put up a film-screen in one of these halls in the presence of the dead man, who had asked for a three-hour film of his concert performances to be shown to his relatives and friends before the funeral. (He was a tap-dancer.)

The scenario for Alik's funeral was comparatively simple: no religious service had been requested and no gravestone ordered, even though Robins owned a decent granite workshop. The mourners had, however, paid for a place in the more expensive Jewish part of the cemetery. It was a crappy plot, admittedly, right up against the wall, with no path running to it.

The ceremony had been arranged for three o'clock. By ten to three, the lobby in front of the hall was packed with people. The present Mr Robins, the fourth incumbent of this thriving family concern which had never experienced recession, was a handsome old man with a Levantine appearance. He was intrigued. He believed the mourners at the ceremony could tell one everything about the deceased, and he found this psychological game one of the most attractive features of his profession. This time he had difficulty in determining the client's property status or even his nationality, indicated unambiguously, it would seem, by the family's desire to bury him in the Jewish part of the cemetery.

The crowd included several black people, rarely to be seen at Jewish funerals. To judge from their clothes they were from the artistic world. The face of one old man looked familiar, and Robins had the idea he was a well-known saxophonist; he couldn't put a name to him but he had seen his face on TV and in magazines. Also present were a group of South American Indians. The white guests too were a complete mixture: solid Jewish couples, some superb Anglo-Saxons, evidently wealthy gallery-owners, and numerous Russians, respectable citizens and out-and-out scoundrels, who were also evidently rather drunk. A fourth-generation American, Robins had his roots in Russia, but along with the language he had long ago dropped his romantic attachment to this dangerous country and its crazy people.

A most unusual client, Robins thought, he must be a musician; he had even made a detour across the funeral building to take a look at him.

At exactly three o'clock Nina appeared in the doorway of the building, accompanied by Fima. Everyone took a deep breath, and let it out again. Her renowned gold and silver hair fell to either side from beneath a black silk hat with a wide veil. Above her short black dress she had thrown an ankle-length coat of translucent black toile. Her shoes were huge, seventies-style platforms with faceted heels.

The gallery-owners groaned in ecstasy. "The best costume design in the history of time," one whispered to the other. "It's gorgeous. Alik always had stunning taste. If he'd gone into fashion we'd have had a designer of genius, rather than a passable artist."

"She's a remarkable model," agreed the other. "I noticed her three years ago."

"She's old now," the other said sadly.

Fima's pale-blue work shirt had symmetrical spots of sweat under the armpits. On his bare feet he wore sandals. As he led Nina in, he experienced sharply contradictory feelings of pity for the poor woman and revulsion for the role he was forced to play; he had little taste for amateur dramatics, and collecting the money for the funeral during the past two days had cost him a lot of bad blood already. Since Alik's death she could remember only that he had got better, and that he was no longer alive. These two concepts would be unable to coexist in normal human consciousness, but in her little head, set brightly on its long neck, everything had changed place like a pattern rearranging itself behind the glass screen of a kaleidoscope, and now the pieces lay in a pleasing new order, separate and in no way interfering with one another.

The words "death," "he has died" and "funeral" rang constantly in her ears, but they didn't penetrate this invisible screen; there was no place for them in the new pattern which had formed in her mind.

Why had they brought her here? It had to do with Alik. Alik loved her to be beautifully dressed, and she had prepared herself carefully, giving much thought to this outfit she was wearing for him now.

She walked on through the crowd of people without recognizing any of them. In her left hand she held to her chest a small black lacquered purse resembling a three-layered bagel. In her right she clasped the thick stalks of some lilies, which trailed their haughty white-and-green heads along the hem of her transparent coat.

The throng parted before her and the doors of the hall swung open. Without slowing her pace, she walked on. Behind her everyone followed in a widening triangle. There were far more people than were usually accommodated in this hall, and most of them carried flowers.

At the end of the hall stood the catafalque, and on top of this was a large open white box shaped like an eau-de-cologne bottle. Inside the box lay a vividly made-up doll looking like a red-haired teenager, with a small face and a little moustache.

A man resembling an ageing television newscaster was already opening his mouth as Nina swept past. Clearly displeased at being upstaged by this extravagant widow, he stepped back.

Lifting her veil, she leaned over the coffin and gazed at the badly sculpted puppet, made from some terrible, unrecognizable material, and she smiled a small smile of recognition: this was instead of Alik, she decided.

She raised her head, and the gallery-owners standing next to her noticed a single black line carefully drawn down the center of her face, from the part in her hair through her neck and disappearing into her low-cut dress.

"What class!" whispered one.

"Ladies and gentlemen!" intoned the newscaster.

It was a literal, word-for-word translation of the usual

graveyard routine repeated beside the crematorium ovens by the fat lady in provincial black crimplene suit on the other side of the ocean.

The coffin was customarily driven to the grave in the hearse by the attendants. But the plot was in such a crowded part of the cemetery that they had to carry it, stepping on other people's graves as they went. Some thirty metres from the plot, the path stopped abruptly leaving a strip of earth a foot or so wide. The men walked ahead and formed a chain up to the excavated grave, and the white canoe sailed on, swaying perilously over their heads as it passed from hand to hand to its last resting-place.

Nina stood by the pedestal of someone else's gravestone, next to the fresh pit, where the earth had been neatly piled up in pink baskets. The powerful August sun drove a light breeze from the ocean, tugging at the black toile of her outfit and ruffling her faded-precious hair like a sail.

Irina stood in the middle of the crowd. She had said goodbye to Alik a long time ago. Now something else tugged at her: she had found a father for her child. She hadn't had much to do with it in fact, they had found each other. She just had to put cash into it—rather a lot of cash, which she wouldn't get back. The grave too had cost quite a bit. But her little girl had had a beloved father, and this was his grave. Irina grinned: she had forgiven him for everything, but she hadn't forgotten. She had given birth to her daughter in a paupers' hospital while he was making love to Nina or that other heifer, Valentina, standing beside her now but half a step behind, knowing her place. Irina could never decide if Valentina was a devious bitch or just a good lay. How spiteful I've become, she thought. Alik, Alik, everything should have been different . . . But it hadn't been, and that was all right.

In this secluded part of the cemetery by the fence were numerous vertical gravestones; each horizontal was surrounded by vertical relatives, as though standing on one leg. The square, angular inscriptions giving the place of birth bore memories of clay slab and reed pen, all mixed up with a funny, gothically accented English, as though the stones carried in them the tastes of these long-gone people.

Alik's closed coffin rested on the adjacent grave. Robins, who had hurried up to honour his unusual client with his presence, commanded the diggers with a conductorly flourish to lower it down. Valentina whispered something to Nina, who opened her lacquered purse and removed the packet of earth. Moving her lips, she scattered the earth over the coffin in pinches, as though putting salt in soup. The gravediggers leaned on their spades.

"Wait, wait!" came a shriek. Behind the mourners' backs there was a sudden commotion. After much pushing and scuffling Gottlieb finally burst through, followed by a large number of bearded Jews, around ten in all. The party was rather late; they had poured out of their bus and had instantly got lost, since each had his own idea of where the cemetery office was. Now, pulling on their prayer shawls and phylacteries, treading on the women's toes and pushing aside the men, they uttered the first words of the *Kaddish:* "May his great name be magnified and sanctified in the world that is to be created anew, where he will quicken the dead, and raise them up unto life eternal . . ." They chanted in their sad, shrill voices, although almost no one but Robins knew the meaning of their ancient lamentations.

"Where did these ancient Hebrews come from?" Valentina asked Libin.

"What do you mean? Gottlieb brought them."

What they didn't realize was that Reb Menashe had decided to take on himself the care of this poor "captive child."

The suspicion dawned on Valentina that the Jews were a little too theatrical; maybe they were from one of the small theatres in Brighton Beach. We must ask Alik, she thought, and instantly realized what a multitude of things she had nobody to ask about now.

The funeral prayers were said, it didn't take long. Then the people at the front stepped back from the grave, and the ones at the back trickled forward. The mountain of flowers grew until they reached Nina's waist, and she stroked each flower, making a strange little house or mausoleum of them and smiling, so that people were now reminded of an ageing Ophelia.

Everyone began to move away. The Jews pulled their prayer shawls off their black, sun-charred suits. They were now at the back, but Nina waited for them and invited them back to the wake. The oldest of them, whose skullcap was attached to his bald head with sticking-plaster, raised two withered hands to his face and spread his yellow fingers, saying sadly: "My child, Jews don't sit and eat after a funeral, we sit on the earth and fast. Although it's very good to drink a glass of vodka too."

They walked back across the cemetery in their steaming black suits and climbed into their minibus, on which were emblazoned the words "Temple of Zion" in dark-blue letters on the white.

TWENTY

Maika, Lyuda and Gioia hadn't gone to the funeral. Maika was busy hanging Alik's paintings. She pulled out the old ones, brushed off two years of dust and wondered where to put them. All at once, like a kitten on the seventh day, her eyes opened and she could see them clearly: this one here, that one next to it, that one above it, take that one away . . . Nothing had to be decided, she had only to look at them and they arranged themselves beautifully and intelligently for her.

"I'm going to study art," she decided, forgetting that she had already dedicated herself to Tibet last week.

The paintings she liked best were the small and medium-sized ones, but one large work begged to be displayed on the end wall. She called Gioia and Lyuda over to give her a hand, and they hung up the three-metre canvas which for five years had stood with its face to the wall. There was a lot going on in the picture, possibly too much: an autumn party with grapes,

140

pears and pomegranates, dancing women and children, jugs of wine, distant hills, a man walking under an awning . . .

Lyuda sliced cheese and sausage and made salads. Gioia dreamily laid out special dishes of quasi home-made Russian-Jewish food from the emigré grocer: herring, pies, meat in aspic, the salad known by Russians as Olivier salad and by everyone else as Russian salad.

The guests arrived all at once and in a large crowd; the service lift bore them up in three shifts. About fifty people sat around the table, made from boards and various bits of timber; the rest took their plates and glasses and wandered around like guests at an American cocktail party. It seemed strange that this concentration of people could produce such a feeling of emptiness.

The Washington gallery-owners were also present. They walked around the studio as though at an exhibition, examining the paintings with a dissatisfied air. Ten minutes later, before the drinking started, they kissed Nina's hand and took their leave.

Irina watched them go without pleasure. They still hadn't given Alik his money or returned his paintings; she would definitely have to proceed with her lawsuit against them.

Faika turned out to be one of those experts on ritual who are invariably to be found at weddings and funerals. She poured a glass of vodka, covered it with a piece of black bread and set it on a plate. "For Alik!" she cried.

This was how things were supposed to be done.

At the table people murmured expectantly; there were no loud conversations or splashes of separate voices, just a monotone hum and the jingle of glasses. They poured the vodka.

At that moment Maika appeared at the door. She was

pale, with a swollen mouth and pink nostrils, and she was wearing a black teeshirt with an orange-yellow inscription. Her sweaty hand gripped the plastic box in her pocket; now it was time for her to take it out.

Nina perched on the arm of the white armchair, although no one was sitting in it. Fima stood, raised his glass and started to say something.

"Listen everyone!" Maika broke in.

Irina froze: she could expect anything from her strange little girl, but not a speech.

"Listen everyone! Alik asked me to give you this!"

Everyone turned to look at her; her face was crimson, like reagent paper during a chemical reaction. Next minute she squatted on her heels and pushed a tape into the cassette-player which stood on the floor. Almost immediately, without a pause, Alik's clear, high voice rang out: "Boys and girls! My Pussy-cats and Cuckoos!"

Nina gripped the arm of her chair. Alik's voice went on: "I'm right here with you! Pour the vodka! Let's drink and eat, like we always do!"

In this simple, mechanical way he had broken down the eternal wall which separated him from them, casting a pebble from that other mist-covered shore and slipping away from it for a moment, stretching out a hand to those he had loved without recourse to the crude magic of necromancers or mediums, moving tables or restless plates.

"There's just one thing I beg you, no fucking tears, okay? Everything's fine, just as it should be!"

Gioia sobbed loudly. Nina sat as though turned to stone, her eyes bulging. The women, ignoring Alik's request, simultaneously burst into tears, and a few of the men allowed themselves to join in. Fima took from his pocket the checked rag he used as a handkerchief.

It was as if Alik could see them: "What's wrong with you people? No tears, I said! Drink up! Mud in your eye! Nina, drink to me! Teeshirt, stop the tape a moment, darling!"

There was a pause. Maika didn't press the button immediately, only after Alik's voice rang out again: "Drink up! That's better!"

She wound the tape back.

They drank standing up, without touching glasses, and the vast emptiness which comes after death receded a little and was filled by a sort of deception, but to their surprise it was filled nonetheless.

Irina leaned against the door-frame. She had already done all her weeping for Alik, yet something still tugged at her. What had been so special about him? Was it that he had loved everyone? But how had that love showed itself? Had he been a good artist? But surely if you didn't sell, it meant you were no good? He had been an artist in his life perhaps; yes, he had lived as an artist. So why hadn't she lived as an artist? Why had she pushed boulders uphill, overcome all obstacles and earned a pile of money? Because you weren't with me my friend, she thought. Where were you?

"Have you drunk up?" Alik spoke again. "Please, everybody get well and truly smashed. Enough with the sad faces, why don't you dance? Yes, I know what I wanted to say: Fima and Libin, if you don't make up your stupid quarrel today you'll be in the shit. There's so few of us, so few. . . . Drink to me, both of you, and quit quarrelling!"

Libin and Fima, boyhood friends who had once played in the same yard together, looked at each other across the table and smiled at Alik's belated curses. They had already made up during the hot months of summer. In the crowds and excitement of the past few days, with the tanks, the shooting, the coup in Moscow, remarks directed at no one in particular had landed in the right place, and the old resentments had melted away.

"They're not touching glasses, they're not touching glasses!" Faika twittered.

"Wait, they've got paper ones." Valentina poured the wine into glasses and they knocked together clumsily, with a muffled ring.

"Here's to you, old roughneck!" cried Fima.

"Here's to the brassière!" Libin said, and both remembered the white brassière with large bone buttons and wire clasps sewn on with thick thread, which they had seen as boys in Kharkov after the war, in the life before last.

"My friends, I can't thank you, because no such thanks exist," Alik's voice went on. "I worship you, all of you, especially the women. I'm even grateful for my damned illness. If it wasn't for this I'd never have known how good you are. No, that's a stupid thing to say, I've always known. I'd like to drink to you. To you Nina, bear up! To you, Teeshirt! To you, Valentina! Gioia, to you! Pirozhkova, I love you. Faika, thank you Pussy-cat, you took some wonderful photos. Lyuda, Natasha, all of you. Men, to you! There's just one thing—I want this party to be happy. That's all, fuckit."

The tape turned, rustling slightly. There were no more words, just a few wheezing gasps. Nobody drank. Everyone stood silently holding their glasses, listening to the convulsive gulping for air and the Indian music bursting on to the tape from the street below.

Everyone strained their ears hoping to hear something else of importance, and it turned out that it wasn't quite the end: the lift clanged, a door banged, then Alik said, "Okay Teesh, stop the tape," in an everyday, tired voice without a trace of pathos. There was a click, then silence.

The merriment didn't happen at once. For a while things were too quiet. Alik, as usual, had done something unusual. Three days ago he had been alive, then he had died; now he occupied some strange third position, and everyone was in a state of grief and shock about it, although they didn't hold back on the alcohol.

People came and went from the table carrying plates and glasses, coming together in groups and moving away again. There had never been such a mixture of people. Alik's musician friends came, along with several people whom no one had seen before; it wasn't clear where he had picked them up or how they had learnt of his death. The Paraguayans stood in a solid phalanx, led by their leader with his dark-pink scar and craggy, handsome face. A Columbia University professor talked animatedly to the driver of the garbage-collection truck. Berman fancied Gioia, but pressures of work meant he hadn't touched a woman for over two years and he wasn't sure if he should let the genie out of the bottle now. If he had known what Alik knew he certainly wouldn't have contemplated it, for not only was she a virgin, she was also the scion of a noble Roman family which was mentioned by Tacitus.

Nina asked someone to get a grey box down from the attic. Inside were priceless treasures, sent over long ago from

Russia via diplomatic friends: this was the first jazz to make its way behind the iron curtain and back. Among the ancient heavy black pancakes were homemade ones, on x-ray plates, and a few brown spools with the first tape recordings.

Only Alik knew how to dance the tango properly, whose complicated steps, heady swoops and swooning falls led so logically in the fifties to rock and roll.

Now Libin took Alik's place with Nina. He stepped out jerkily, twisting and turning, but he didn't have the necessary artistic languor to give the tango its special aroma. The black saxophonist fancied pale Faika, and she felt torn: like most Russian emigrés she was a racist, yet the man before her was one undoubtedly American product she hadn't yet tried.

The party slowly came to life. Those who were offended left. Berman and Gioia left too. Both had made their decision but were unsure if it was the right one. Gioia was shaking with nerves, terrified that she would become hysterical when the moment came. But everything happened beautifully, and by morning each realized that they hadn't lived all these years alone in vain.

Shortly after ten o'clock the landlord came back, accompanied by a flustered Claude. He had informed his boss of his tenant's death, and after waiting a couple of days, leaving what he considered to be a decent interval, the man arrived to inform Nina that the apartment was to be vacated on the first of the month.

When he came up to her to hand over the document in person, she mistook him for someone else. Kissing him she told him in Russian to find himself a glass, and absent-mindedly dropped the letter on the table, from where it fell to the floor. It didn't occur to her to pick it up. The disgruntled landlord shrugged and left; Claude tried in vain to persuade him that he was present at a traditional Russian wake.

Someone put on an old tape, a humorous version of a Moscow jazz hit from the late fifties:

> *Moscow, Kaluga, Los Angeles*
> *Joined in a big collective farm*
> *On the hundredth floor in St Louis*
> *Russian Vanya plays a riff . . .*

Everyone smiled at this old music, Americans and Russians alike, but it meant much more to the Russians: because of it they had been attacked at meetings, expelled from schools and colleges. Faika tried to explain all this to her partner the saxophonist, but she couldn't find the right words; how could you explain it, when everything was so sad? Suddenly, a sort of hilarity would break through, something sweet, a kind of physical joy, yet their hearts were still heavy with sadness. This was what drove them on.

Lyuda already felt so much at home in this place that after a few drinks she forgot where she was and jumped up to run over to her neighbour Tomochka to pour her heart out, forgetting that Sredne-Tishinsky Street wasn't around the corner.

"Mum, you're so funny when you're drunk. I've never seen you like this, it suits you." Her son pulled her away from the door.

Maika went over to Irina and touched her shoulder.

"Let's go, I've had enough."

Her face was stern.

Lean Irina took off down the street after her doughy

daughter, and suddenly realized that something was happening between them, had happened already maybe: it was as if the tension of the last years, when she had constantly felt her little girl's sullen dissatisfaction with her, had dissolved and disappeared.

"Mum, who's Pirozhkova?" Maika asked.

This was the first time she had heard this surname.

Irina didn't answer at once, although she had long prepared herself for this moment. "I'm Pirozhkova," she said at last. "We had an affair when we were very young, at about the same age you are now. Then we quarrelled. Years later we met up again. It didn't last long, and in memory of the meeting Pirozhkova kept his baby."

"Good for Pirozhkova," Maika nodded. "Did he know?"

"Then, no. Later, maybe."

"Good parents," groaned Maika.

"Don't you like them?" Irina stopped walking; she was still hurt by the things her daughter didn't like.

"No, I do. Other parents are worse anyway. He knew of course." Maika's voice was weary and adult.

"You think so?" Irina was startled.

"I don't think, I know," Maika said firmly. "It's terrible that he isn't here."

The hum of Russian and English voices was broken by a sudden shriek. Flinging her black Chinese slippers off her feet, Valentina ripped off the top button from her yellow shirt with a gesture reminiscent of a dashing guitarist striking a chord. A shower of buttons fell to the floor as she strode out shuffling her thick pink ankles, her face shining like a lacquered Russian doll, and sang in her high, seductive voice:

> *Hey there boy!*
> *Stir your tar*
> *I'll mix my dough*
> *We'll mix and stir together!*

She slapped her thighs and nimbly stamped her feet on the dirty floor. She had spent her student years in a whirl of field trips through northern Russia, collecting fragments of living Russian speech in Polesye, around Arkhangelsk and the upper reaches of the Volga, studying her bawdy folk-songs the way others study the nucleus of a cell or the movement of migrating birds. She remembered ditties by the thousand, in all their innumerable variants, dialects and intonations, and she had only to open her mouth for them to come pouring out, alive and unspoilt, as though she had just come from a village party:

> *Spit on my iron,*
> *My iron is hot . . .*

She scattered little lumps of burning coal around her, and her dark heels drummed the floor as though stamping on them as they fell from the stove.

The Paraguayans were beside themselves with joy, especially their leader.

"What kind of music is this?" the saxophonist asked Faika, but she had no words to describe it and merely said, "It's Russian country music."

Shortly before Valentina's folk number, Nina had walked dramatically to the bedroom, her head high, her back straight. As she sat on the edge of the bed in the semi-darkness she heard the jingle of glass, and realized that she wasn't alone. Squatting in the corner with his back to her she saw Alik, going through the remaining bottles, looking for something.

She was unsurprised, but didn't move from her place.

"What are you looking for, Alik?"

"There was a small bottle here, of dark glass," he grumbled.

"There it is," she replied.

"Ah, so it is." He stood up, happily clutching the dark bottle to his old red shirt.

Nina wanted to warn him to be careful, because the mixtures left disgusting brown stains. But he walked right past her, and she saw that he really was fully recovered and was moving exactly as he used to, with his old light step, slightly disconnected at the knees. There was more. As he passed her he touched her hair, not carelessly but in the old special way he had, parting his fingers like a comb, lightly pushing them into the roots and drawing them back from her forehead to the nape of her neck. And again she saw her cross hanging on his chest, and she realized that everything was all right.

"I must tell Valentina," she thought as her head touched the pillow.

She wouldn't have been able to find Valentina, for Valentina was far away. In the shower-compartment of the bathroom, the squat, muscular Indian was pounding into her with his short, massive organ. She saw his black hair falling over his sunken cheeks, and the livid strip of skin stretched tightly over the scar. Her wrists and ankles felt encased in iron, yet she was suspended, unsupported, hammered powerfully upwards . . . What was happening to her was unlike anything she had ever experienced before.

TWENTY-ONE

The telephone woke Irina in the middle of the night.

"It's probably Nina calling up drunk," she thought, picking up the receiver. She glanced at her watch: it was just after one a.m.

But it wasn't Nina, it was one of the gallery-owners, the one who did the paperwork.

"An urgent matter has arisen regarding your client," he said briskly. "We wish to acquire all the remaining works in his studio without further delay."

Irina held the pause, as she had been trained to.

"Of course, we assume you'll halt all legal proceedings," he went on. "Our relationship will now be reviewed."

One, two, three, four, five . . . Get this!

"Well, in the first place, as regards legal proceedings, that is a matter quite separate from the other issue, and we couldn't under any circumstances connect the two. As regards my client's work, I can discuss that with you at the end of next week after I return from a visit to London in connection with these works," Irina lied, with great professional satisfaction.

She wasn't the least bit tired. Getting up, she walked into the living-room. Two strips of light poured from under Maika's door. She knocked and went in.

Maika, wearing a long nightshirt despite the heat, propped herself up on one elbow and pushed away her book. "What's the matter?"

"It seems Alik was a good artist after all. Those sharks just called and want to buy all his paintings."

"You mean it?" Maika smiled.

"Yes. I'll dig out an inheritance for you yet, my girl."

"You're joking, what inheritance? And what about Nina?"

"Nina's no concern of mine. And we're going to have to work like hell for that money." Irina's face was very tired, and it seemed to Maika that she was ageing, and at night, without makeup, her mum didn't look beautiful at all, just ordinary.

"You know what, let's go to Russia," Maika moved aside, making a place for her on the mattress.

For years Maika hadn't been able to sleep alone, and Irina would hurry from the other side of town so that her unhappy, silent child could bury her head on her shoulder and fall asleep.

Now Irina lay down beside her and arranged her bones more comfortably on the bed. "I thought about that, too. Yes, we'll go, definitely, only let's wait for them to get sorted a bit first."

"Get what sorted?"

"You know, wait for things to settle down a bit, whatever."

"But Alik said if things ever settled down it wouldn't be the same country any more."

"Don't worry, things will never really settle down there . . ."

Irina stroked her daughter's red hair, and for once Maika didn't twitch or grunt.

Well then, Irina thought, it looks like that's the end of that.

New York, Moscow, Mont Noir. 1992–7